THE PRIVATE LIFE OF PLANTS

Lee Seung-U

The Private Life of Plants

A NOVEL

TRANSLATED BY INRAE YOU VINCIGUERRA
AND LOUIS VINCIGUERRA

DALKEY ARCHIVE PRESS

Originally published in Korean as *Singmuldeurui sasaenghwal*
by Munhakdongne, 2003.
© 2003, Lee Seung-U
Translation © 2015, Inrae You Vinciguerra, Louis Vinciguerra

Library of Congress Cataloging-in-Publication Data
Yi, Sung-u, 1959-
 [Singmuldul ui sasaenghwal. English]
 The private life of plants : a novel / by Lee Seung-U ;
translated by Inrae You Vinciguerra and Louis Vinciguerra.
-- First edition.
    pages cm
 ISBN 978-1-62897-116-3 (pbk. : alk. paper)
 I. You, Inrae, translator. II. Vinciguerra, Louis, translator.
III. Title.
 PL992.9.S87S4613 2015
 895.73'4--dc23

                                    2015030140

LIBRARY OF KOREAN LITERATURE

Partially funded by the Illinois Arts Council, a state agency
Published in collaboration with the Literature Translation Institute of Korea
Dalkey Archive Press publications are, in part, made possible through the support
of the University of Houston-Victoria and its program in creative writing,
publishing, and translation. www.uhv.edu/asa/

Dalkey Archive Press
Victoria, TX / Dublin / London
www.dalkeyarchive.com

Cover: design and composition by Mikhail Iliatov
Printed on permanent / durable acid-free paper

The Private Life of Plants

1

"Why are you laughing?" asked the lady of the night, wide-eyed. She was wearing silver lipstick, tight shorts, and an annoyed look. I didn't answer her. It was obvious from her frowning face that she thought I was going to be a difficult customer. But I wasn't really interested in what she thought. I thought that her lipstick color was quite unusual for someone in her profession, but I really didn't think anything else about her.

I was sitting behind the wheel of my car and the woman was standing outside, her face poking through the half-open window. She didn't bend her knees but instead stuck out her rear end. So from where I was sitting it was impossible to appreciate her buttocks. But I did notice her voluptuous breasts inside her loose-fitting T-shirt. And I didn't think I needed to avoid looking at them, so I peered at her bosom while I talked to her. A sequence of thoughts followed: first, it seemed that she was proud of her breasts; secondly, it appeared that she expected me to admire them so she purposely posed this way in order to expose them to me; and finally, if that was the case, ignoring her expectation wouldn't have been the right thing to do. I asked her how tall she was and how old and would she wipe her makeup off, and I then asked her to turn around and to take ten steps. Flippantly, she answered that she was 160 cm tall, twenty-two years old, and that she wouldn't mind wearing no makeup in bed even though she didn't understand why. But she ridiculed my request for her to turn around, grumbling that I wasn't there to choose a fertile mare, and she totally ignored my last request. "Are you gonna do it or not?" she asked, clearly annoyed and pressing me for an answer.

That's when the scene from the movie came into my mind. It was a funny association and I grinned like a cat. But before my smile could be completed, it became a frown.

Where had I seen that movie? It must've been at one of the all-night movie theaters that I used to sleep at in the outskirts of the city. It was a movie made by an Iranian director who had earned some notoriety. I later learned that the director had an odd name—Abbas Kiarostami. As I hadn't gone to the theater to watch the movie but to sleep, I wasn't interested in what it was about. And although the movie had gotten good reviews, that didn't mean all the spectators would be highbrow, since I, too, was in the audience that night. To be honest, I didn't really understand why people were raving about the film. Sitting in my seat in the darkness, all I wanted was to fall asleep. But it was one of those nights that so many thoughts invaded my mind and demanded my attention. Finding it difficult to fall asleep, I gazed absentmindedly at the screen for quite some time.

It was a movie without any action or suspense or even humor. And since it lacked these elements, it was naturally quite boring. But maybe it hadn't been all that dull since I still remember bits of it. Yes, regardless of my disinterest there must've been something about the movie that captured my attention. And who would've ever imagined that the "something" would emerge at such an unexpected moment after hibernating in my memory for such a long time.

In the movie a man in an old car was doggedly searching for somebody to pour dirt over his soon to be dead body. And when the streetwalker, obviously annoyed, asked me whether I was going to do it or not, I suddenly realized that I wasn't so different from the man in the movie, and this made me grin. Searching for someone, just as the man had, I had been driving slowly, so slowly that it looked like I was taking a leisurely ride. Both the man in the movie and I needed someone to help us. But the man had spent the whole day searching. Who knows, it could've been several days. I was much better off—it had only been two hours since I'd left home. I'd arrived to that particular part of town about forty minutes before. And I'd cruised around with the driver-side window half open, scrutinizing the women walking by or leaning against streetlight posts, talking to some of them.

But why hadn't the man in the movie looked gloomy? I asked myself. His composed and cautious manner made him seem more like a company man dealing with an important business matter rather than a person determined to leave this world. *Do I look like him? Do I look like a company man just trying his best?*

My interrupted smile was the answer to my question, a question that did not have a simple answer. Like the man, I knew that there was no reason for me to be gloomy, but at the same time, I also knew that what I was doing wasn't something to be proud of either. The woman couldn't have understood why I was amused but I didn't feel obliged to explain it to her. It would have been impossible anyway.

"What do you think I want to do?" I asked her.

She stared at me for a moment, seemingly confused and searching for an answer to my question before she suddenly became irritated.

"Are you gonna do it or not?" she asked, for the third time. To do or not to do was her only question. As though only those two choices existed. And since there was no alternative, she pressed me for an answer. Yes, it would have been annoying to almost anyone. Except for sophists, who enjoy complicating this world even more, most people would prefer to live simple lives. Hamlet, a symbol of the suffering man, was actually a master of living life in an extremely simplified way. His question is whether to be or not to be. Is that a real problem? Is that all there is to it? How could life be so simple?

I wonder how determined the man in *A Taste of Cherry* (the title of the Iranian movie) had been to kill himself. To do or not to do! Didn't the guy just need somebody to make the decision for him? And wasn't that why he had been wandering about—to find a suicide assistant? His resolve and determination to find someone is understandable if it is seen as a search for a person he can entrust his fate to. He didn't want just anyone to cover his body with dirt. The person he was looking for wasn't just a suicide assistant who could shovel dirt but the magistrate of his fate. And since the probability of finding the right person to carry out his death was fifty percent or less, the guy in the movie wasn't gloomy. The director of the film might've intended to convey the message that no one really wants to commit suicide.

And there wasn't any reason for me to pretend to be gloomy. I wasn't looking for someone to decide my fate. I was just looking for a person to satisfy lust. And it wasn't even my own lust. Being serious and gloomy just isn't like me. And anyway, it would have been unnecessary.

"Get in," I told her, pointing with my chin to the passenger seat, as if I'd finally made a difficult decision. Grinning quizzically, she hopped into the car. Her face beamed with conceit, like she knew all along I would pick her up in the end. Her vulgarity irritated me. But I understood that it was her professional pride. It was natural for her to act this way, this was her job and I didn't want to offend her. I rolled up the car window and drove in silence. Streetlights sped by like shooting stars.

Once we'd left downtown the woman suddenly began prattling. "Men are ridiculous . . . why do guys have to act all shy when things are obvious?" She then crossed her legs. With this move, her shorts rolled up and became even shorter, giving me a fuller view of her round thighs. She was also wearing mud-splattered high heels. I didn't like getting my car dirty but I decided not to let it bother me. Her babbling, though, continued. "I don't understand why you all have to act like you're noble gentlemen while you're roaming around like an animal in heat. Why can't you stop playing games? I'm not saying you're the only man who's ever acted this way . . . eight guys out of ten do it. Isn't it funny that men act as if we were forcing them against their will, that's what I call ridiculous. Maybe you guys think acting that way will make you seem less like animals, but I don't think there's anything animal about it to begin with," she said, glancing at me as she finished her speech. I knew she was expecting me to agree with her, but I didn't respond. So she came to her own conclusion: "Anyway, what's wrong with being an animal? We humans aren't so great . . . we're animals too."

"Why don't you keep quiet and start wiping that thick makeup off your face?" I said, growling at her. I really don't know why I talked to her that way, but it was probably because she'd used the word "animal" so many times and it made me uncomfortable.

As if surprised by my unexpected outburst, she flinched and then studied my face. She soon struck back, as if showing me that she wasn't intimidated by my words. "What's the point of wiping off my makeup?" The woman was making me talk too much and that annoyed me.

"Just do it! And take off those gaudy earrings too," I snarled.

The irritation in my voice was obvious but she continued jeeringly, "What's with you? I'm not your girl."

I shouted back that she didn't have to worry, that I couldn't even imagine her as my girlfriend.

"Why do you have so many petty demands then?" she retorted sharply, her crossed leg bobbing up and down.

Yes, why did I have so many miserable demands? It was because I had a particular woman in mind. I had been thinking of her ever since I'd decided to look for a streetwalker and I'd thought of her throughout the whole evening as I drove down the streets. Thinking of her excited me. Even though I knew that the woman next to me didn't know what was going on in my mind, nonetheless, I was embarrassed by her remark.

"Listen, I drove up and down this street for an hour. Obviously, I've been looking for a woman. And there were plenty. So don't think I didn't see women prettier than you. Why do you think I chose you?" I was being mean but fortunately, or unfortunately, I didn't provoke her.

"Well ... maybe I'm just simply your type? Or who knows, maybe my boobs blew your mind?" she said, laughing. She then stuck her big breasts out toward me. But I neither laughed nor turned my head away from her. What she said could've been true to some degree. She indeed had a voluptuous body and gigantic breasts. But choosing her wasn't based on my own taste at all. Whether I liked big breasts or not had nothing to do with it.

I took an envelope stuffed with money out of my jacket pocket and tossed it to her. Seemingly, this wasn't something new or unusual to her, since she casually picked up the envelope, but after peeking inside she asked in an awed voice, "Is this all mine?" I was not prepared for her reaction but I had no intention of playing into it. Again, I ordered her to take off her earrings and to remove her makeup. I then reminded her that I had bought her time and that I wanted to make sure she understood what that meant.

"I understand, and anyway, they're not difficult things to do," she said. She took her earrings off and put them in her purse along with the envelope and then began rubbing off her makeup with tissue. Marveling at the power of money, I stole glances of her face as its white mask disappeared.

We arrived at our destination before she had completely finished removing her makeup. I must've driven for about twenty-five minutes. Without the multicolored neon signs that had glared out from the downtown storefronts, the streets in this neighborhood seemed dark and desolate. There were few people around and cars sped by without a second glance. Before we even got out of the car, I could smell the scent of grass. Urban and rural were connected in such a way that it was only a twenty-five minute drive out of the city. Through the darkness a motel sign came into view. It read "Eden" and it had the image of steam escaping from a hot spring. The eerie scene reminded me of a haunted castle in some horror movie, but the woman didn't seem to see it that way, which I took as a favorable sign. Her behavior revealed that she was a simple woman and, in addition, as dumb as she was simple. I was confident that I had made the right choice.

"Honey, you got me," she said, in a coquettish manner, clinging to my arm. I brushed her arm away and walked toward the building, steam belching out from somewhere inside. The woman followed a step behind me. Angered at my indifference, she huffed and murmured as if she thought that I was gutless and shy. She had misinterpreted the situation. But I did not correct her.

I got the room key from the front desk.

2

I remained impassive as the woman hissed in anger. She accused me of deceiving her, but it wasn't true. I hadn't. I'd never said that I would be the one sleeping with her. I had chosen her but that didn't mean I would be her customer. And I didn't feel guilty because it wasn't my responsibility to have corrected her misunderstanding beforehand. As far as I was concerned she was in no position to accuse me of behaving shamelessly. I had paid her in advance for her services with an amount that had impressed her. She was now acting like she had been mistreated (like a victim of some kind of fraud!), but I felt that I was being unfairly accused of deceitfulness.

Cursing, she tried to dash out of the motel room, but I grabbed her hair and slapped her hard before shoving her back towards the room. It was a gut reaction and perhaps a bit more physical than necessary, but she didn't leave me much of a choice. Running out of the room right away! She was the one who had broken the contract! She apparently hadn't expected to find me outside guarding the door or that I would be prepared to hit her if she tried to leave. She seemed intimidated by my glare.

"This isn't what we agreed on," she said, pleadingly, while rubbing her cheek. From her tone of voice I could tell that she was now trying to win my sympathy.

But I felt no sympathy for her at all. "What did we agree to that I didn't do?" I asked, still holding her by the hair.

"You didn't say I'd be with another man," she answered, in a shaky voice.

I scoffed at her reasoning. "Did I say I'd be sleeping with you? Think about it. Did I?"

Fearful now, she had lost her will to fight. "Of course you didn't but . . ." she said, her voice gradually tapering off.

"Listen! Shut up and get back into the room! Unless you want your legs broken, like his," I barked. My words seemed to have had their intended effect as she now looked truly afraid. I had assumed that she was a simple woman and a bit dumb, and as much as she was simple and dumb, she was also fearful. I knew that this kind of simple, dumb, and fearful woman would usually be very docile, and my assumption proved correct. Overcome with fear, she glanced at my closed fist and then entered the room, still cursing under her breath.

It was five years ago that my brother lost both his legs. I wasn't living at home at the time. I had been wandering and would go anywhere and do anything as long as it kept me from having to return home. And it was only a year ago that I first saw my mutilated brother. During the Chuseok Holiday (Korean Thanksgiving) one year, sitting alone at work, I became sentimental and had a sudden urge to visit my hometown, and this eventually led to my predicament, if indeed it was one. I was feeling a bit lonely, which brought back long suppressed memories. I wanted to visit my hometown but I wasn't planning on seeing my family and I wouldn't have if I hadn't seen my mother's minister, who told me about my brother. When I saw my legless brother it brought back humiliating memories and terrible feelings of guilt. Then one night during my visit my brother's missing legs appeared in my dream but in the dream they were my legs. That night I decided I had to move back home for good.

I had the dream on the third night after returning home. In my dream I was walking into darkness. It was so dark that I couldn't see anything in front of me; I felt as if I were disappearing into the blackness as I stepped forward. And, while moving through the darkness, it gradually became thick and sticky. At first it was like walking through fog, then through a swamp, and finally through quicksand. Naturally, it became difficult for me to continue walking. And it soon felt like I was trapped in some kind of adhesive substance. As soon as I managed to lift one foot, the other one became trapped in the sticky darkness. Looking for a way back, I turned around and saw nothing, only black. "Is anybody there?" I shouted in despair. And, of course, no one answered. Soon something happened that caused me more despair. For some reason when I attempted to take another step I felt something was missing. A chill shot through my spine. From my thigh down, my left leg wasn't there. I immediately looked at the other leg and saw that it was also gone. Stung by fear, I screamed loudly. A man whose face wasn't visible soon emerged out of the darkness and began speaking to me, and he appeared to come from outside of my dream. "Are these your legs?" the man asked, holding a pair of legs in his hands. They were strong and beautiful legs, muscular and hairy. And I don't know how, but I immediately knew that they were my brother's. And I also knew that the man holding the legs without exposing his face was my brother. As if to confirm this, his face appeared in front of me. But as his face came into view, his legs disappeared. I screamed again. And my scream tore through my dream and I awoke.

The first thing I did upon waking up was check to assure myself that my legs were there. The second thing I did was walk to my brother's room, where he was sleeping, and lie down next to him. Lying there, I knew that I wouldn't be able to leave him.

3

I refused to sacrifice my life in order to take care of my brother. I don't think my rejection of such a sacrifice is something that I should be ashamed of, though I know that it isn't something to be proud of. But I'm simply not that kind of person. What caused me to move back home was the guilt I felt whenever I recalled memories of my brother and the compassion I felt for my parents who eventually had to let go of all the dreams and expectations they'd harbored. My mother was gone all the time and my father hardly spoke. One of the few things my father did was water the plants that filled the garden. I rarely heard a word from him. Mother once said, sadly, that he must've developed aphasia after my brother's accident.

I had never thought I would be the kind of son my parents could be proud of and it wasn't my intention to attempt to take my brother's place as the favorite. I was simply shocked at my brother's condition and the shock diminished my resolve to leave home again. But it had certainly never been in my plans to help my brother satisfy his carnal desires. It was a sad and humiliating chore. I was disgusted by the animal sex drive that sometimes overcame his maimed body. I could not suppress my revulsion toward my brother but I was heartbroken over what my mother had been reduced to: forced to roam the brothels with her son on her back. It would've been different if I hadn't seen it, but once I saw it, I just couldn't ignore it. Outraged, I shouted at my brother, saying he would be better off if he just killed himself right then and there. I held my mother and began crying.

It all began one night. After dinner I was lounging in the living room watching TV when my mother carried my brother out of his room on her back. My father was alone in his room playing ba-duk. If I listened carefully, I could hear the black and white stones being placed on the board. And sometimes I heard my father forcefully slamming stones down on the board. But I was so accustomed to hearing him play the game that my ears would unconsciously block out the sounds.

Hoisted onto my mother's back, my brother seemed annoyed and resistant. "Mother, I don't want to do this," he said. I was sitting on the sofa when his eyes met mine, but he quickly turned his head away from me. He then seemingly gave up and became silent as he hid his face in Mother's back, his legless trousers dangling down.

"Where are you going?" I asked casually. Neither Mother nor my brother answered. Instead, there was a tense silence that clearly indicated no further inquiry was welcomed, so I didn't ask anything more. Mother put my brother in the back seat of her car and then got in the driver's seat. Since she usually asks me to drive, I became suspicious and I knew that something strange was happening. I couldn't just stay home and wonder so I got into a taxi and followed them.

Since I didn't have the slightest idea where they were going, I was very surprised when my mother's car stopped at the Lotus Flower Market. The city's red light district was for some reason called by this name and as if by the prostitutes' own choreography, scantily clad women vulgarly chewed gum and strutted about soliciting men as they passed the shacks divided into small booths lit by red lights. Why would Mother come here? And with my brother on her back? It was bewildering.

I watched my mother and her son, his face buried in her back, until they entered one of the shacks lined up along the street. My brother looked sullen but Mother's gait showed confidence and familiarity with the area. It didn't look like this was their first visit to the Lotus Flower Market. The women cleared the way for the mother and son as they passed by, seemingly a familiar sight. I appeared to be the only one who was embarrassed. Like a negligent actor who gets on stage without rehearsing, I stood there helplessly, not knowing what to do. I looked sheepishly around at the women, not because I was interested in them but because I wanted to assess their opinion of the mother-son pair that had just passed by. Their faces revealed pity as well as disgust, which saddened and upset me. I didn't know where my emotions would take me and I felt the urge to run away and escape from it all. At that moment a streetwalker approached me, grabbed me by my arm, and whispered, "Wanna have a good time, honey?"

Brushing her hand away I asked, "Who's the woman, the one who just entered that shack?"

"Oh, do you mean the mother with her son?" she said immediately, indicating that she knew them. "Isn't it pathetic? But they have their story too. Anyway, who cares, come on in, I'll make you happy." She grabbed my arm and dropped the subject. I asked her to tell me everything she knew about the mother and son. But the woman seemed perplexed as to why I would want to know more about them. "It's just what it appears to be . . . what else do you need to know?" I pressed her for more information, asking if they came there often. She answered that they showed up now and then and said, somewhat sympathetically, "It's a sad story when you get to know it. I heard that her son is very intelligent. But unfortunately he lost his legs while in the military. I feel sorry for him . . . but the mother is something else. I've never heard of a mother helping her son in such a way. It's an odd thing for a mother to do, isn't it?" Pulling her hand off my arm, I left the Lotus Flower Market. I felt nauseous. *No mother should do something like that!* My inner rage was so strong that I felt my heart would explode.

I must've walked around for some time. Finally, I went into a sidewalk bar stall and began to gulp down soju. I wanted to get drunk, but the more I drank the sharper and more acute my worries became. I couldn't simply get drunk and forget about it. So finally, without any specific plan, I went back to the market. And Mother was still standing in front of the brothel.

With her eyes closed and her head leaning against the glass door of the shack, it all looked familiar to me, since it was the same pose she had taken as she had leaned against the iron gate of the prep school when I applied and when I took my entrance exams. She had been praying then. She had done this twice for me and I knew that she would have been willing to do it many more times. But she didn't get another chance. I'd escaped the hellish prep school in the lonely northern province of Gyeong-gi, where students were confined in prisonlike cells, controlled like soldiers in boot camp while eating, sleeping, and studying. This regimen was advertised as some kind of revolutionary education, with the school even boasting it was a "Military Academy." That was the first time I ran away from home.

What did she pray for in front of the door while her eldest son was satisfying his lust, a lust erupting from his mutilated body? And I wondered what kind of prayer was permitted by her god under such circumstances? But I soon concluded that her prayer was spurious; no god existed who would answer such a prayer. I felt that she was an abomination. And I approached her, close enough so that my chin almost touched her shoulder.

I then called out to her, "Mother!" My voice sounded like an animal growling. The sequence of her actions: opening her eyes, lifting her head, turning around toward me, all seemed to occur in slow motion. And I'll never forget the distress in her face. She wore the expression of someone forced to witness an unbearable scene. I felt that I was the one forced to witness something unbearable, that her consternation was really mine. But worthy of her reputation as a clever manipulator, she skillfully handled her emotions. Anyone who knew my family said that we got by based on her maneuverings, and nobody in my family denied it.

"Oh, you're here," she said, seemingly unperturbed, as if we had planned to meet in this very spot. She was so unmoved that I even wondered for a second whether I had forgotten about an arrangement we had made. "But it would've been much better if you hadn't shown up," she added, gazing at something in the distance. It was if she had known I would come sooner or later. Then she ordered me to leave, saying it was about the time my brother would be coming out of the shack. Her voice sounded firmer and more resolute than ever. Yes, her voice was stern, more so than I had ever experienced.

"Mother!" I shouted. I tried to remain calm but my voice was trembling with emotion.

"I don't know how you ended up here, but you definitely didn't make the right decision. And if you don't leave right now, you'll make it even worse. So leave," she said as she turned her head away from me.

Just then the glass door opened and a young woman's face emerged. "We're done," she said, and then she put her head back inside. Mother opened her eyes and looked at me. Her face was pleading with me to leave. She was chasing me away. The desperation in her eyes told me that I shouldn't be there when my brother left the brothel. She appeared determined not to enter the shack to get him unless I left first.

I wanted to comply with her wish. I knew that if I didn't leave, my brother would never be able to look me in the eye again. But as if possessed by a demon inside, my rational mind was overcome with emotion. Logic is indeed weaker than impulse. As if to prove this, my body suddenly sprang forward. Brushing my mother aside, I pushed open the glass door. Yes, impulse is also quicker than logic. Determined not to let my mother block my way, I forced my way into the shack. Faced with a series of doors, I flung open the first one. On the bed that took up almost the entirety of the small cubicle there was a man facing the wall, huddled up like a caterpillar in a cocoon.

I sprang at my brother. Turning his body around so that he would be facing me, I grabbed his throat. I was behaving like an animal, huffing and snarling. My brother's eyes welled up with tears and he appeared to be in shock, but I didn't care. I shook him by the neck, shouting at him. But overcome by violent emotions, my words didn't form sentences. Rage sprang out of my mouth as I yelled, "Look . . . you . . . miserable worm!" I then wailed on about human dignity before shouting, "End it all . . . do it . . . just disappear!" My broken sentences mingled with my tears. If Mother hadn't rushed in and pulled me away I don't know what would've happened. She slapped me with all the strength she could muster. She seemed to know that it was the only thing she could do to calm the angry animal inside me. I collapsed against my mother's bosom and began to cry. She didn't push me away nor did she pat my back to comfort me. I wondered if she was also crying. I couldn't lift my head to face her so I'll never know.

4

In reality, it wasn't purely by chance that I ended up following my mother and brother to the Lotus Flower Market. I had been following my mother for some time at the request of a new client. Was he playing a prank on me? I wasn't sure but it made no sense. This was no lighthearted joke, it was serious, with malicious intent behind it, which is why I felt so uneasy.

I had been hired to tail my mother. It sounds ridiculous but it's true. So what I witnessed at the market wasn't the result of my being simply curious or my having some kind of psychological disorder. As I said, it was my job.

One day a man, without identifying himself (I didn't yet know who he was), called in response to one of my flyers. He wanted to hire me as an investigator and the person he wanted me to report on was my mother. He wanted to know her every move. It was an absurd request. I almost asked my new client if he knew that the person he was asking me to follow was my mother. It was ridiculous, whether he knew it or not. So I tried to think of it as some kind of prank being played by a friend. I tried to discern whether my client's voice reminded me of anyone I knew but I did not recognize it and after a moment of silence, I asked him how he'd found out about our agency. I'd said "our agency" but there wasn't really any office or any other employees. It had been about five months since I'd installed the phone line in my room and started distributing leaflets. I had finally realized that I couldn't continue loafing around the house forever and I had the idea of starting a personal assistance agency, the only kind of work I've ever done.

During the time I was away from home I had worked for quite a long while as a messenger at an agency called The Runners. It didn't pay much but they let me sleep in the office at night. My job was mainly running errands for our clients to district or registry offices and to train stations. The work somehow fit me, a loafer. As I was a person starting up a business alone, what attracted me to the work was that most of the contacts with clients were made over the phone and thus I didn't need any office space. And the experience I'd gained at The Runners must've given me some confidence. So once I'd decided to do it I immediately set up a phone line and named my business Bees and Ants, a name I greatly admired, and I had stylish business cards printed up.

The grand opening of my business consisted of handing out my business cards to my family. Mother doubted whether it would make any money but she was glad that her son was finally attempting to earn his own living. My brother showed disdain at my starting such a business and my father, as usual, didn't show any interest at all. He wouldn't have even blinked an eye even if I had brought home a strange woman who already had a couple of children and said I was going to marry her.

As one could easily have predicted based on my grand opening and the size of the business, I didn't have many clients and therefore I wasn't in any position to be picky about them. Even under such circumstances it was still preposterous to tail my own mother. Yes, no one can ever know what will happen in the future, which is one thing that makes this world more bearable, but I for sure never imagined that my future held such an assignment. So it was natural for me to wonder from the start who the mysterious client was.

The client paused and then said he had seen an ad in *The Pigeon*, a free newspaper distributed in Seoul and the surrounding area. It was true that I had put an ad in that paper. I had tried more formal advertising after getting only a few calls from the leaflets and small signs that I hung everywhere—at malls, on electric poles, and even in public restrooms. So I'd decided to invest some money in advertising in the free local papers. I had little expectation, though, about the effect the ad would have, since I'd seen that this kind of advertisement had never brought in much business for The Runners. And I'd never imagined that because of the ad I would get an assignment to spy on somebody. If only the target hadn't been my mother, it would've been a pretty interesting job.

"May I ask what your relationship is to this person?" I asked casually, which must've revealed my interest in identifying who he was. He then asked if it was necessary for him to answer my question. I knew I couldn't justifiably insist that clients provide personal information, especially a client who wanted me to tail somebody. That kind of client always tries to maintain strict confidentiality. People wanting to know about other people's business are ironically the ones most reticent about their own private lives. I felt that if I pressed him for an answer he would've hung up the phone and that would've been the end of the case. I would've not only lost a sizable amount of money but also any chance of discovering something about this man who wanted to spy on my mother. I just couldn't let that happen.

I told him it would be helpful to have as many facts as possible but that I would respect his right to privacy. He then fell silent so I asked how and when I could contact him with my findings. He said that he would call me regularly to receive whatever information I had gathered. I then told him about the fees for my services and gave him my bank account number. With the risk involved, I explained that my fees would need to be quite high, but the price didn't seem to bother him. I asked him to wire the money into my account on a weekly basis and he agreed to do so. "As soon as the first deposit is made I'll begin the case," I informed him in a businesslike manner before hanging up.

The man immediately wired the exact amount I had asked for into my account, and by so doing, he officially became my client. Therefore it was because of a stranger that I followed my mother and brother to the Lotus Flower Market and witnessed the abominable scene there. What I had done as a son was disgraceful and I felt miserable about it. When he called me later that night, and I couldn't help but speak roughly to him.

"Who are you? What do you want from me? What the hell do you want?" I yelled at him.

But he didn't reply. And this made me even more furious, so I announced that I was quitting the case. The man seemed amused and I think I even detected a laugh as he proceeded to inform me that the contract couldn't be broken by one side. "You got paid for this and you know you've got to finish the job," he said. Unable to control my anger, I began to shout at him, but he had already hung up.

5

For about a week after the fiasco at the Lotus Flower Market our whole house was silent. I felt suffocated by the dead calm. We all avoided each other. As usual, Mother left home early in the morning while I slept late. And each morning our maid prepared breakfast for me, but I always left the house hurriedly without eating much. Some days I had to work and other days I didn't. I went out when I had work and I also went out when I didn't. And since I didn't want to face my brother, I waited until after midnight to return home. It was so late that no one was around to let me in, which was fine with me because I always carried a house key in my pocket.

Not everyone was in bed at that hour. And it was obvious when my brother was up. Often I would hear him typing at his keyboard. He was always doing something in his room but his door was closed at all hours so I had no idea what was going on in there. As a matter of fact, the four bedrooms we occupied were almost always closed shut. We rarely trespassed upon each other's space as no one wanted that to happen. Mother was the only one who sometimes broke that unwritten rule. We indeed lived like strangers. But nobody resented this nor complained about it.

I had a talk with Mother a week after the incident. Sitting alone one night in our dark living room, she was the one who initiated the conversation. It was after midnight and, as usual, I was about to sneak into my room after unlocking the front door and entering the house when suddenly, in the darkness, I heard my mother ask me to have a seat on the sofa. It seemed she had been waiting for me. I did as she asked and sat down across from her. As if to calm herself down, she paused for a moment before beginning to speak. "Did you come to see me today?" she asked. I shook my head. "Somebody told me they saw you near the Dandelion today."

Her voice was soft and calm, as if she were trying not to disturb anything in the dark room. The Dandelion is the upscale restaurant that Mother runs. She had begun working there when she was young and was now the owner.

Embarrassed and not believing what she had said, I asked her how she'd known I was there. It was true that I had gone to the Dandelion. Even though I had lost my temper and yelled at my client, insisting that I was going to drop the case and that I would not give him any more information on my mother, I still couldn't help being curious about what on earth that bastard hoped to find out about her and whether she really had any secrets. Anyway, I had nothing else to do. So that day I had in fact prowled around outside the Dandelion. But before long I began to think it was futile and I started to feel guilty again so I made my way home. I wondered how she had found out I was there.

She then asked me why I hadn't come in if I'd needed to talk to her. She seemed to think I had gone to her restaurant to speak to her. I was relieved by her misinterpretation. I shook my head. Honestly, I had nothing to tell her.

She shrugged her shoulders and began talking anyway, "Your brother . . ." Since we hadn't yet spoken about the scene from the previous week, she appeared to have decided to bring up the matter herself. "Your brother isn't in good health," she said. That was nothing new. "And I think you know that it's not only his physical health but also his mental state. Usually, he's fine. But sometimes he totally loses control without any warning, and at those times . . ." she paused for a moment. I could feel that she was trying hard to rein in her emotions. She then lowered her voice, as if being cautious not to let my brother hear her. "At those times my heart shatters into thousands of pieces as I remember how your brother was once such a bright and healthy young man. I must've done something terrible to deserve this fate . . . having a son maimed." Her shaky voice came in waves, revealing that it was indeed difficult for her to control her emotions, something unusual for my mother.

"I know that he was always your best hope, and your expectations were very high," I finally managed to say.

Mother didn't deny it. It was true. Her favorite had always clearly been my brother. But I didn't think her favoritism unfair or my brother's privilege undeserved. He had earned his place through his winning traits. And thus I thought it right that he was the favorite. Especially when his superior talents were compared to my inferior ones, it was logical that he should receive the majority of her affection. From early on inferiority was my everyday food and drink. Compared to my brother, I didn't do well academically or as an athlete. And I wasn't better looking than him either. All this made me believe, starting from a very young age, that the world wasn't fair. After failing my college entrance exams, I tried to join the army in an attempt to escape from the situation, but when I was rejected even by the military, I was eaten up by despair.

"I can't believe you're astigmatic . . . it would make sense if your brother was," Mother said. And, unfortunately, I wasn't too dumb to detect her derisive implication that I didn't study hard enough to have developed such an eye condition. Yes, my brother was superior to me in everything; he was superior to many people. From very early on he had always been my mother's pride and joy. And I had empathy for my mother, whose perfect son had one day been plunged into such a terrible situation. I wasn't able to relate to most people but I was certain that I could fully empathize with her sadness.

Even considering all of the facts, however, I still wondered whether it was proper for a mother to take her son to a brothel. Maybe she thought she was being a good mother. But could this be called love? Here, my understanding reached its limit.

Her soliloquy continued. "When I saw him in the hospital in that condition, it was hard to bear and I just wanted to die. But I couldn't . . . instead, I became numb," she said.

"I wasn't there," I said, gloomily.

"No, you weren't," she repeated, confirming my words.

It was true that I hadn't been around when my brother returned after losing his legs in an explosion during a military drill. And when he left for the army I wasn't home either. I heard only later that he had been drafted into the military. And within one year the accident occurred.

"He's usually okay, but when he has a fit, he tears his clothes, claws at his body until it's all black and blue, and bangs his head against things . . . it couldn't be worse. He then takes off his clothes and crawls all over the house, doing terrible things. I'm sorry to say it, but . . ." For a moment she stopped talking and held her breath. But she resumed speaking, clearly wanting to finish what she had begun, "He masturbates, spraying his sperm everywhere . . . it's just unbearable. Once the insanity passes, he becomes silent and limp and soon falls asleep. I took him to a psychiatrist who told me many things. For example, he said that your brother's fits seemed to erupt from his repressed libido. And he said that when the body's control mechanism is disrupted the accumulated negative energy will eventually explode and this is what we call having a fit. He said that a fit expresses itself in different ways, and for some reason it's expressed as sexuality in your brother. He then asked me if your brother was married. So I told him that he'd had a girlfriend before the accident but he didn't marry her. The doctor then said, 'A man's sex drive is an urge toward physiological discharge. Without one, it overflows. One way to solve this problem is to find a proper way to discharge your son's sexual needs before he has a fit and becomes violent.'"

Mother's voice faded. And with this, she even lowered her head, making it difficult for me to hear what she was saying. She seemed to feel the need to explain the incident at the Lotus Flower Market to me. She might've wanted me to understand that her trip to such a place wasn't only based in maternal love but also on my brother's mental health needs.

"And so you had the idea of taking him to that place?" I asked her.

"I couldn't think of any other way," she said.

"Do you think it helps him?" I asked her.

"Your brother was at first ashamed and humiliated by it," she said. "But he eventually adjusted to it, since he was fearful of having a fit, and he knew there wasn't any other way for him to get help. And yes, it worked. And that's why we didn't stop. And that's . . ." Her speech sounded like a confession.

"I got it Mother. Okay, I'll take over from now on," I said to her, rather impulsively, and then I stood up. I didn't want to hear about it anymore, but I realized that had probably been what my mother wanted me to say. I can only assume that at first she believed it would be better if I didn't know about it, and so she didn't tell me, but once it was no longer a secret, she must've thought that I would be much better at dealing with the situation. It no longer upset me at all. Actually, I felt good about it. I could finally be of some use.

6

The approach I took to my brother's treatment was simpler than my mother's. Instead of carrying my brother on my back to the red light district, for example, I took him to a motel on the outskirts of the city. There, I got my brother a room and afterwards found a woman and brought her to him. All the women complained after seeing him, but that was something I had anticipated. I'm not a particularly kind person and I didn't feel the need to tell the women beforehand who they would be dealing with. I doubted that there were many women who would still come with me after hearing the whole story which is why I couldn't be up-front with them.

Burying himself deep in the passenger seat, my brother was speechless. We were on the way back home from a motel. I could imagine the turbulent emotional waves surging inside him. His turmoil consisted of humiliation, self-condemnation, loneliness, inferiority, and defeat, and they seemed to be boiling inside him. Believing that I should respect his feelings, I remained silent.

"I'd like to stay out a bit longer," he said in a calm voice as we neared our house.

"Isn't it rather late?" I asked, turning to look at him. He remained silent. I drove the car toward the royal mausoleum which was located near our home. It was about a ten minute walk from our apartment, twenty minutes in my brother's wheelchair, and two minutes by car. I knew that my brother liked to visit this place. But when we arrived he refused to enter the area where the king's tomb was located. A narrow path flanked by hedges skirted the tomb. It was twisty and bumpy with large trees arching upwards from the sides blocking out the whole sky. Once you were on the path you felt like you were in a cave. My brother had always liked that path and now and then he asked me to take him there. I would drop him off at the entrance and he would ask me to pick him up in two hours. I always asked him if he wanted me to push his wheelchair for him, but he always shook his head, saying it was unnecessary. It was obvious that he liked to go there alone. He was a punctual person so he was always waiting for me at the entrance when I arrived two hours later. Sometimes I arrived a little early and I sat watching him make his way back along the curved path. Usually, he concluded his visit at around sunset.

This was the first time that he wanted to take the outing at such a late hour. But I didn't feel I should ignore his request. I stopped the car at the entrance to the mausoleum and sat him on his wheelchair. This time he didn't ask me to come back in two hours to pick him up. So I slowly began pushing his wheelchair down the path.

The night air was cool and the light from the streetlamps was no match for the stubborn darkness. Rumbling along, the wheelchair made its way through the dark. After turning a corner, the light from the street no longer reached us and the blackness deepened. I wanted to turn around where the streetlights ended, but my brother's silence urged me onward. The wheelchair rolled over the path, its yellowish ground guiding us through the dark forest.

I was well aware that the chill I felt wasn't caused solely by the cold night air. All along the path the trees thrust themselves up toward the sky, propelling us into an eerie world. I felt as if we were slowly being sucked into the intestines of the night and that we would soon fall into a black hole at its core. I was scared. Suddenly, I heard the rustling of a wild animal. Nearby, night birds screeched. This made me all the more nervous and I was reminded of Hansel and Gretel. The dark fear and deep loneliness that the abandoned children in the fairytale experienced had always struck me. And I felt that my brother and I were also abandoned by the world. I began to imagine that the witch who lures children to her cookie cottage would soon appear before us as it's well known that the night forest is a haven for witches. The night forest is a world of its own with inexplicable logic and laws, dominated by witches and ghosts; a grim reality that conceals itself behind the so-called real world of the day. The witch's cookie house, where Hansel and Gretel were taken, seemed to me a fairytale metaphor for a black hole.

At some point I realized that I hadn't ever walked the path so far before, much less at night, and although I wasn't sure what my brother felt, I for one didn't like it. I had always thought that I would have liked to walk the path with him, but I hadn't expected this: the late hour and the fear. I began to worry how much further he wanted to go. I almost told him that we should turn back before the witch's cottage appeared. But I couldn't open my mouth—his silence was impenetrable. I decided to defer to his judgment, and I let this resolution grow stronger than my fear.

"The path ends here," my brother said. I was surprised because I didn't immediately recognize his voice, gripped as I was by the night's phantoms. I was relieved that he had broken his silence. Distracted by fear, I'd continued to push the wheelchair forward quickly through the darkness and it seemed that we were now much deeper in the forest than I had thought. "We can't go further. This is where we stop," he said. His voice hung heavily in the damp night air. "I can imagine the dense forest beyond the hedge," he uttered. He continued talking, as if to himself, "I can imagine the tall trees competing to possess the sky and the deep caves that must be somewhere out there. And I can imagine shrubs and wild grasses entwined with each other and with the birds and insects and animals and the earth. And if I keep going deeper into the forest maybe a gigantic ash tree will be there, propping up the sky. I wonder if I would see all that if I went deeper and deeper into the forest. I always wanted to go further in. Once there, I would want to become part of the forest. I would want to touch the huge ash tree that not only props up the sky but also props up time." His words contained strong emotion and seemed to express his heart's hidden desires.

"Well, I'll take you there sometime," I said, trying to sound casual. But I soon felt that my response seemed frivolous and shallow next to his heartfelt speech. My face was burning and I knew it must be bright red. I was thankful that he couldn't see me in the darkness.

"Do you see that tree over there?" he asked, pointing with his finger, as if he hadn't heard what I had said. I wasn't able to make out a single figure in the darkness that covered the forest. The trees had lost their individual identities and had become a mass of blackness. *What tree? What was he seeing?*

"Are you saying you can actually see out here?" I asked him cynically. But he ignored my question.

"That's a pine tree," he said, nonchalantly. "It's tall, with a wide trunk and thick bark. But look at the tree right next to it. This one is totally different from the pine tree. With its thin, slick trunk entwined around the pine tree, it reminds me of a woman with dark, smooth skin. Do you know what the tree's name is?" he asked.

"No. What is it?" I responded. I still couldn't make out any specific tree in the darkness, but I decided to go along with him. I was also curious as to what had incited this nighttime trip through the forest. I wasn't sure if my brother's growing interest with nature, in direct proportion to his increased disinterest in people, should be encouraged. "Snowbell," he said, suddenly naming the tree.

I repeated the name. It was a tree I had never heard of and therefore I could not even visualize what it might have looked like. He said that the tree with the strange name was standing right in front of us, though I still couldn't see it. I knew that he was familiar with the place and had no doubt seen the tree many times, but I hadn't and so I couldn't comment on it.

"This tree's slick trunk reminds me of a naked woman's slender body," he said. His voice sounded otherworldly. "But the really fascinating thing about it is its flowers. Since it's May, they'll soon bloom. The white flowers look like silver bells, with their faces hanging down toward the ground. And when I sit under the blooming tree I feel like I can hear bells ringing," he said. Like an anchor plunging into a deep ocean, his voice sank into the dark forest.

I didn't know what to say and I didn't really feel like talking anyway. I was thankful that he had begun speaking because it helped distance me from the sinister forest, too much like the one where things had gone badly for Hansel and Gretel.

My brother's entranced voice continued on, sounding like it was rising up from the depths of the ocean. "But I wonder why the slender snowbell tree winds around the pine's thick trunk. To me it doesn't look like a random occurrence." He then let out a short sigh.

I still didn't understand what he was talking about. I could only imagine his intention (for example, he felt a need to justify his lust), but I really wasn't sure. The problem was that the tree, which reminded him of a slender, naked, smooth-skinned woman, was still invisible to me. My curiosity became irrelevant as I felt the wheelchair's handles begin to shake. The shaking seemed to originate from his shoulders but that couldn't be right since shoulders can't move voluntarily. What was causing both the wheelchair and my brother's shoulders to tremble was his sobbing.

"What to do with this humiliating body . . . with this sadness inside me?" His voice penetrated into the blackness that hid the snowbell entwined around the pine tree.

I had heard him clearly, but I pretended that I hadn't. I was embarrassed, but pretended I wasn't. "I should come here during the daytime to see what the snowbell tree looks like," I said. I'm not good at camouflaging my feelings but I cleared my throat and spoke. "I'm scared. Let's go home." And without waiting for his answer, I turned him around. I pushed the wheelchair along the dirt path. Through the wheelchair's handles I felt his sobbing for some time, but I didn't say a word all the way home, and he didn't either. And again I thought of Hansel and Gretel, abandoned in the deep dark forest.

My brother and I entered the house and went into our rooms as if nothing had happened.

7

The following morning I took a walk alone on the path and by the time I'd returned home I was determined to convince my brother that he should take up photography again.

At a relatively quick pace I had walked from the tomb's entrance to the end of the path. It was longer and more snakelike than I'd remembered. It also had some steep graded sections, which made me wonder how I had been able to push the wheelchair so easily. The night before, when I had wheeled my brother to the end of the path, he had spoken about his profound passion for the forest. He'd talked excitedly about the snowbell snaking around the pine in such a way that it was as if he were censuring his own lust. "It doesn't look like a random occurrence," he had said. And listening to him I too had become somewhat excited.

I wasn't sure what had drawn me back there. Maybe I wanted to see the slender snowbell that supposedly curled around the pine tree or maybe I wanted to see the forest itself, with its deep, dark cave and trees and grasses and vines all entwined together, making up one body, a forest where, after a long journey, I would find a gigantic ash tree propping up the sky. Whatever the reason, I walked alone down the path. It was about ten o'clock in the morning, and either because it was too early or too late for a walk, I didn't see anyone else.

Reaching the end of the path, I stopped walking and looked at the forest. It was a sunny day but, nonetheless, the forest seemed dark. And it wasn't just simply dark. A tangible energy pervaded the darkness. I thought I heard ethereal whispers coming from the forest. Suddenly, I felt giddy. I realized I was experiencing the forest's mysterious and bewitching power.

And then I saw the snowbell. I had never seen this kind of tree before but I recognized it immediately. Its appearance was striking; my brother's description hadn't been an exaggeration at all. To be honest, I hadn't believed much of what he'd said the night before. I'd thought that his turbulent emotions must've hindered his ability to describe things objectively. But the tree in front of me proved that I was wrong. It indeed looked like a naked woman, agile and slender. And her slick body coiled around the pine trunk in a sensual manner, like a naked woman hugging a man. I felt that if I dug down to the tree's roots, I would find them curling and snaking even more freely and passionately than the trunk. I felt strange, as though an ominous prophecy that I had wished false had now come true. "The snowbell," I gasped.

I'm not sure whether that was the moment that I thought of my brother and photography but it was at some point during my walk in the forest. I knew that after what I'd done to him all those years ago I was in no position to offer advice of this nature. But once the idea had come into my head, I became preoccupied with it. I went into my room after lunch to mull it over. I knew he would think it brazen of me to bring up his photography. But I was certain that photography would help him and therefore I concluded that I should set aside my pride, for his sake.

I started out by telling my brother that I had taken a walk to the end of the path and had watched the forest sunk deep in silence and dark shadows and had seen the snowbell tree that coiled around the pine. But my brother didn't respond immediately. It wasn't unusual for him not to respond, so I continued speaking. I told him that the tree looked exactly as he had described it the previous night, and so even though it was the first time I had seen it, I immediately recognized it.

He didn't express any interest in my remarks but simply responded that the snowbell's fruits are poisonous. "I heard that in the old days people caught fish by sprinkling its poison into the river," he muttered.

Not wanting to get off topic, I decided to get straight to the point. "Don't you feel like taking photos when you see such beautiful things, like the snowbell and the pine tree? Why don't you take up photography again?" He neither looked at me nor answered.

My brother's reason for giving up photography was that he could no longer trust its value as a faithful record of things. Or maybe it would be closer to the truth to say that he felt betrayed by his photos, which he had taken with such devotion. At one time photography had been more than a hobby to my brother, but he hadn't considered it an art either. For him, photography had been something that showed the objective truth of a time and place. Photos were the most accurate eyes and the most honest voice. Of course, a photographer has his or her own viewpoint or perspective when taking photos. No person can be absolutely objective and so all facts must reflect the views and beliefs of the person who does the recording. Photographers reveal their inner selves through the different angles and focal points they choose. My brother believed that the photographer should take photos from an ethical angle and with a focus on morality. That had once been my brother's philosophy on photography. And this was the very reason he didn't consider photography to be a form of art. As far as I know, he has never wanted to be an artist.

I remember the days when my brother was always on the streets with his camera. It was a time when Seoul often teemed with demonstrators and the air was filled with tear gas. His eyes watering and nose running, he devotedly clicked his shutter. He took photos of the police throwing tear gas bombs and wielding their clubs while charging against protesters. He snapped shots of protesters throwing firebombs against the police shields, and photos of grimacing passersby, running for safety to avoid exploding tear gas bombs. His camera also caught the torn T-shirt of a student, his neck gripped by a policeman, military police leaning against a bus to nap, rifles stacked like a pile of garbage next to them, and mounds of stones that female students had collected for the demonstrators. He bought countless rolls of film, took many photos, and developed all of them himself. His room had been filled with those photos, and I gained quite an accurate impression of what was happening outside my home just by studying them. His photos were more accurate and reliable than the newspaper articles. Photos communicated the facts powerfully and more clearly than the written word. And I think that it was then that I developed the habit of only quickly scanning newspapers.

Some photos were horrific, some sad, and some were frightening. And without fail, all of them evoked a deep response from the viewer. Often it was wrath or hatred or despair. I understood that my brother's photos represented what he sought through photography. I agreed with the practical value of photography that had an ethical angle and moral focus. I realized that his photos were a record and, at the same time, they were more; they were also weapons. The accurate recording of facts was a powerful weapon. His photography was indeed not just a hobby or an art form but his way of fighting. Photography had given purpose to his life. Many of his photos made their way out into the world, published in crudely printed leaflets. And my brother, as a devoted photographer, numbered each photo with the date and place it was taken. He did this not only to the photos that were published but to all his photos. Sometimes he added captions under specific photos, such as, "June 14, Kwanghwamun Underpass, demonstrators fled to the underpass for safety and the police exploded tear gas bombs inside."

Through the albums of photos that occupied a whole bookshelf in my brother's room, I could relive the history of our times. Although he and I had rarely talked to each other and he didn't like me going into his room, he didn't mind me browsing his albums. And on rare occasions he had even taken out some photos and explained them to me. There were photos that he felt needed some explanation, but in my opinion they spoke for themselves. When this happened, I always listened to him attentively. I felt honored when my brother patiently explained his photos to me; it meant he was treating me as an equal. But it didn't always happen this way. Most of the time he ignored me, reminding me that he was on a different level than me.

8

I count it as the beginning of the end: a woman thrust herself between my brother and me. I know he would take issue with this way of putting it and I can't deny that when judged by the actual order of events, it was me who interfered in their relationship.

Her name was Soon-mee. She had short hair with bangs, never used any makeup, and often wore white T-shirts that made her fair complexion seem even fairer. Her smile formed cute little lines around her eyes and her laugh reminded me of springtime sunshine. She sang beautifully, too. But above all, she was my brother's girlfriend.

When I would hear her clear voice radiating out from his room my heart would ache with envy and jealousy. My brother loved the songs she sang and I can only assume that she must've also liked singing for him. There are many recordings which serve as evidence of her talent. I still have one of her tapes in my collection. Accompanying herself on guitar, some of the recordings were done in my brother's room and some were done elsewhere. She not only sang but also wrote her own songs. One of these songs was "Take My Heart My Photographer." It was obviously a love song to my brother. He would listen to her songs whenever he was home. And when he wasn't home, I listened to them. Our house was always filled with her music.

When did it start? When did my heart begin to burn feverishly for her?

When I returned home after the first time I'd run away my parents no longer pressured me to study. Realizing that my inability to adjust to college prep school had caused me to leave home, they were afraid that I would flee if they pushed me into a similar situation again. It was nothing new for my father, a taciturn man from birth, not to say much, but my mother became extremely cold toward me. And my brother, busy roaming the streets with his camera, also paid little attention to me. He hardly said anything, even when I returned home after being away almost a month. I wondered whether my brother even noticed that I had been gone.

Anyway, at that time I was freer than I had ever been, and I became more aware of myself and my place in life. Strangely, as I prepared for my third try at the college entrance exam, I suddenly had the desire to study hard. It was an unexpected change in me, and it made me feel slightly uncomfortable when I stopped to think about it but I threw myself into preparation for the exam. It was around then that I first met Soon-mee. It was the end of April, when the white cherry blossom flowers shed their cheerful petals. One day I happened to answer the door when she rang the bell. Her hair was short, she had no makeup on, and she wore faded jeans and a white T-shirt.

When she said "Hello?" her shining teeth were exposed and for a moment they brightened up the whole porch. I'm not sure what I asked her but she mentioned my brother's name and then asked a couple of questions in a row: "You're Woo-hyeon's younger brother, aren't you?" and "Is your brother in?" I told her honestly that I didn't know whether my brother was home. She then asked me in disbelief but jokingly, "You don't know if your brother's home? How can that be?" I felt like she was scolding me, but I wasn't offended. "Maybe he's working on his photos. Can I check in his room?" she asked. She brushed past me and made her way to his room. Her gait was agile and spirited. That was the first time I met her.

Was I attracted to her from that first encounter? I want to say no. I certainly didn't have feelings of jealousy. It was clear that she was devoted to my brother. From that first meeting I couldn't have anticipated that her feelings for my brother would soon begin to cause me great pain. Could it have been her singing that seized my heart, stirred my emotions, and upset my sense of balance, until I was finally unable to think clearly?

One day I overheard a conversation coming out of my brother's room. "Sing for me," he told Soon-mee at one point. I pressed my ear against the door and eavesdropped on them.

She giggled as though she were being tickled. "Okay, I'll . . . I'll sing . . ." she said, still laughing. I waited for her to begin. As if he knew that I was outside his room listening attentively, my brother said something in a low voice. I couldn't hear what he had said but I could make out her response. "How can I sing then?" she asked, but her voice was even louder and full of laughter, so it was obvious that she didn't mind who was listening.

Right then my brother hissed, "Shhh." Her voice soon subsided a bit, but for a while their laugher continued to flow out of the room.

I have to admit that I wasn't simply passing by my brother's room that day; I remained lingering near the door. I told myself I was just curious but I understand now that it was more than childish inquisitiveness. It's hard to explain but I had a deep yearning to hear her sing. I believed that I understood and admired her songs even more than my brother did. My heart swelled at the thought of a woman singing for the man she loved; it seemed so beautiful and romantic. How could I possibly have left such a scene?

Presently, she began to sing. It was a familiar melody and her voice was alluring. Then, unexpectedly, jealousy began to burn inside me. It was absurd, utter nonsense! I wasn't in the position to be jealous of anyone! But despite all logic I was helplessly consumed by a raging envy. Simply imagining myself in the place of my brother, sitting right in front of her, put me into such an ecstatic state. Nothing could be done to calm my burning heart. From that day forward I suffered in my love for her. Whenever she was with my brother in his room, whenever their conversation and laughter seeped through the door, whenever her songs floated to me on the air, I became restless. Unable to study, I would pace back and forth in front of his room.

Finally, Soon-mee began to appear in my dreams. And in my dreams she only sang for me, just as my heart desired. She sang a beautiful, entrancing song and I kissed her guitar, soft and warm as a human body. Her singing transformed into arms, her arms wrapped around me, and the guitar's melody became her tongue as it slipped into my mouth. And in another dream, I entered the hollow of her guitar. Inside, it was cozy and warm and just dark enough. Following a mazelike tunnel, I reached a cave where I curled up as comfortably as a baby in its mother's womb. And those nights, I always had wet dreams, without fail.

9

Day by day, as my secret love for Soon-mee grew, my hatred toward my brother also grew. I was delusional, holding tight to the belief that no man could be blamed for whom he loved. As opposed to hating someone, to love someone is honorable and it is even more honorable to continue loving someone under impossible circumstances. I clung to this abstract ideal. Each love exists in a unique world of its own where it is born, recognized, and experienced. For this reason every love is special. But no love can exist in a vacuum. I failed to take heed of the circumstances surrounding my love. I purposely closed my eyes to them. But I soon discovered that new desires are born where truth is ignored. I asked myself why my love for Soon-mee should be seen as dishonorable. The answer to the question I posed was easy to answer: it was because of my brother. I never asked *Why on earth did I end up loving my brother's woman?* Instead, I asked, *Why does my brother have to be an obstacle to my love?* All my thoughts revolved around me; I was the center and there was no one else. I believed that there had never been love before my love; any love that had come before mine wasn't real. My brother's love had not come before mine because it wasn't as real as my love and therefore it didn't even exist. As illogical as it sounded, I was serious, dangerously so. Yes, my love was a serious and dangerous one.

One day, when my brother, my rival, was out, I decided to sneak into his room. My heart beat quickly and my face burned with shame. I wasn't sure what I expected to find, I just wanted to see some evidence of their love. I didn't expect to come up with anything that would end my brother's relationship with Soon-mee, but I wasn't going to walk away empty-handed either.

Upon entering his room, it was as if something shimmered in

the air in front of me. Overwhelmed with giddiness, I brought my hands to my head. The scent that permeated the air, the smell of a woman, almost toppled me to the floor. It was the smell of Soon-mee. Her scent filled the room, overpowering any traces of my brother (did my brother have a certain odor? I really didn't know). The smell made me both excited and sad. Searing with jealousy toward my brother, who even possessed her scent, I violently rummaged through his belongings. I found a photo of her in a pile of photographs. She was smiling brightly under a blooming cherry blossom tree, I immediately picked it up as though the photo were mine and I had just come into the room to retrieve it. When my eyes fell on a tape labeled "Soon-mee's Songs for Woo-hyeon" my heart felt as if it would burst. I picked it up and left the room. I then placed her photo in my wallet and the tape into my cassette player. I put my headphones on and listened to it, then took her photo out of my wallet and looked at her face for a long time.

The following day my brother said he'd noticed something unusual in his room. Tilting his head, he asked me if I had been in there. Acting innocent, I said no. "That's strange, then where are they?" he said. He rummaged through his desk, bookshelves, and drawers. He then searched in the living room and the kitchen and even my parents' rooms. I knew he was looking for Soon-mee's photo and the tape. Feigning ignorance, I put my headphones back on as he continued searching the house. Soon-mee's voice flowed into my ears. Her singing was sweet, and it was made extra sweet by the fact that I was secretly enjoying her tape right in front of my brother, who was madly searching for it. My triumphant mood expanded to the point that I felt Soon-mee belonged to me and not to my brother.

From that day, my brother locked his room whenever he went out and I took this as a sign that he didn't trust me. But with my bundle of extra house keys, I could still get into his room whenever I wanted. I loved to smell her lingering aroma in the air and examine the traces of her mixed in with his belongings. By accident, I uncovered his other photos in his room and I took my time to look through them. They were photos of the city's smoky sky, tear gas bombs and fire bottles zipping through the air, interlocked rows of protesters, faces distorted in pain, police clubs raised in the air, hands waving flags, and mouths screaming slogans. The photos taught me what was truly happening in the city; they made me aware of the kind of air I was breathing and of the world I was living in.

I didn't question my brother's reasons for taking such photos. But I wondered why he didn't take photos of Soon-mee. I hadn't found a single photo of her in all of his albums. The photo I had stolen from his room hadn't been taken by him. I admired my brother's devotion to photography and his belief that it was the only truthful record of events but I failed to understand why he hadn't taken a single photo of his beloved. I felt sorry for Soon-mee for loving such a cold man.

But regardless of what I felt, Soon-mee made my brother another tape. I found it one day as I was searching his room. For a moment I had a strong urge to take it, but I knew my brother would notice, so I decided to leave it. But not before listening to it. As Soon-mee sang, my brother's playful comments and laughter could be heard in the background. I realized then that the tape had been recorded in his room. After the first two songs, there was a long interval between songs. A conversation between my brother and Soon-mee had been recorded.

"You're my nymph," my brother said.

"You're my beast," Soon-mee replied, giggling.

"Sing the song 'Take My Heart My Photographer,'" he told her.

"Bingo, I was just about to do that one, my photographer. But is there someone outside?" she asked.

"Don't worry. My mother isn't home yet and my father is taking his walk, and Ki-hyeon is studying in his room," he answered.

After a pause, Soon-mee asked him, "How are you and your brother doing?"

"In what area?" he asked.

"In every area," she answered.

He then tried to change the topic by saying, "I don't exactly know what you mean but what I do know is that you can just ignore him."

Laughing, Soon-mee then said, "I can't just ignore him, there's something about him."

"What do you mean?" my brother asked, turning serious.

"I'm not sure," she responded, "but I just have this uneasy feeling about him . . . maybe it's in his eyes when he looks at me."

I held my breath at her remark. "What do you mean . . . his eyes?" my brother asked, in a voice tinged with anxiety and suspicion. It seemed like his question was directed not only to her but also to himself.

In my eyes? I repeated to myself. What about my eyes? What does she mean—something in my eyes? And when she said that what she saw made her uncomfortable did it mean that she had read me correctly?

"I have this uneasy feeling when he looks at me, but maybe I'm too sensitive . . . I don't know . . ." she cut her answer short, as if unsure of what she was sensing, or simply afraid to speak up.

"I noticed something too," my brother said. And this remark of his made me nervous.

"Oh well, maybe it was just my imagining. I'll sing now. Why don't we sing together, 'Take My Heart My Photographer,'" said Soon-mee, as she began playing her guitar.

"Remember, you're my girl, understand?" said my brother, but his voice was drowned out by the guitar's melody.

They then began to sing. "I gave my heart to you. But here I've stood for such a long time without even a glance from you. How much longer will I stand here waiting for you? Before I melt away, before I melt away, like snow without a trace, take my heart, my photographer . . ."

Breaking into my brother's room became habitual. I wanted to stop doing it (I didn't think it was something honorable at all), but the room tempted me, and the temptation was too strong to resist. I often stood up without thinking and found myself with the bundle of house keys in my hand, walking toward his room. I went in there almost every day. Lying down, surrounded by her fragrant odor, I would listen to her songs. At first my heart would gallop like a race horse and then become as calm as a deep lake on a windless day. My initial state of agitation compounded by my absurd jealousy could have led to foolhardy actions. But as it turned out, it was the tranquility that Soon-mee's songs lulled me into that would prove more dangerous. One day, listening to her songs in my brother's room, I fell asleep. And this turned everything around.

My brother woke me up. I suppose I knew it was bound to happen, sooner or later, but when it finally happened, it was much worse than I had imagined. I was half asleep and bewildered when I was awakened with a kick. A moment of confusion passed before I comprehended the situation. I noticed then that Soon-mee had stopped singing and then, recognizing the gnarled face glaring down at me, I realized where I was. Embarrassed, I rose quickly. But my brother continued kicking, causing me to fall back down. "You maggot, what the hell are you doing in my room?" howled my brother, hissing with anger. I knew he had a right to be angry, so I didn't argue or fight back, I just curled up on the floor. He also seemed to think that he had a right to be angry, so he continued to kick me.

"I knew there was something strange going on with you. I always had this feeling that someone had been in my room while I was out. Things were missing too ... and I knew no one in this house except you would do such a thing. So what do you think you're doing here, you idiot? You should know yourself. You know what you really are—a loser." He hurled his harsh words at me without giving me any chance to reply. I wouldn't have known what to say for myself anyway. I was just thankful that he'd come home alone, without Soon-mee. The thought of her seeing me this way was even more horrifying. Although I was the most insignificant and lowly member of the household, I didn't want her to see me being beaten like the dog I was.

10

I'm not exactly sure when my brother first suspected my love for Soon-mee. But the day he found me sleeping in his room must've confirmed it. And when he'd said "You should know yourself," he was also warning me, in an indirect way. If he admitted that I had feelings for Soon-mee, his girlfriend, it would hurt his pride, since he would be forced to acknowledge that I, his insignificant brother, was his competitor in love. I understood why he couldn't speak about it directly.

But my love for her was too strong to be deterred by a few kicks from my brother. Rather, some kind of competitive spirit began brewing inside me, fermenting uncontrollably. My brother had made a mistake; the incident in his bedroom only made me determined to free my love from its dark cave. I had to let Soon-mee know how I felt about her. My strange passion gripped me tightly and inflated my self-confidence to a dangerous degree. I loved her so much that I was certain she must love me too. I was a hostage to my own fantasy and passion. And it was this reckless, delusional state that drove me to visit Soon-mee's home. It happened on a Sunday. A huge demonstration had been planned that day in the center of the city. I had heard that at the march opponents of the administration would launch a massive campaign to remove those in power. My brother set out early that morning with his camera. He wouldn't miss it for anything.

I took a bus to where Soon-mee lived just outside the city limits, one of those neighborhoods I never visited. I had copied her address from a letter she had sent—to my brother, of course. When I found it in our mail I had to fight my urge to open it; instead, I just wrote down her address. Maybe I thought that someday I would write her a letter.

The complex she lived in was huge but it was well organized, so finding her apartment was easy. A woman who seemed to be Soon-mee's mother spoke to me over the intercom. Her tone of voice hinted that she was somewhat less than thrilled about a strange man coming to see her daughter but despite any reservations she might have had, she gave me information about her daughter's possible whereabouts: Soon-mee wasn't in but she might be at the library but she wasn't sure, and she had no idea when she would be back. I said that I'd wait for Soon-mee outside, and she once more told me that she had no idea when Soon-mee would be home. "I'm okay," I said, so that she would understand that I was willing to wait regardless of how long it might be. I strolled around the apartment complex to kill time and then sat on a bench to watch the children playing at the playground. To be sure I hadn't missed Soon-mee, I rang her doorbell every hour. Around dusk, I finally slumped down to the ground in front of her apartment building.

When I rang the doorbell again at around nine o'clock, the woman who I thought was her mother seemed shocked and asked me if I had been outside, still waiting, all that time. I sensed fear in her voice, but I didn't understand why. I didn't see any reason for her to be afraid. "Since it's getting late, would you come back another day?" Her voice sounded extremely polite, as if she were asking me a big favor. I again said, "I'm okay." But I didn't realize that my reply probably alarmed her even more; it didn't even occur to me that my behavior could have provoked anxiety or fear. I felt that my passion was my own problem and while I knew it might harm me, I never imagined that it would frighten anyone else.

It was around ten o'clock when I felt something strike my shoulder. I was still squatting on the apartment steps. I don't think I had been sleeping, but, nevertheless, I felt like I had been jerked out of a slumber. "Are you the fellow who came to see Soon-mee?" A tall and sturdy man in a suit asked as his hand continued to press down on my shoulder. When I lifted my head to look up, I saw an imposing face glaring down at me. I tried to get up but he applied more force to my shoulder. He didn't look like he was making much effort to hold me down but I couldn't move at all. "Is this the guy you talked to?" he asked, turning his head away from me and look-ing behind him. A woman nodded. She was peeking halfway out from behind the door, as if she were afraid to leave the building.

"Who are you? What on earth are you doing here?" The man tightened his grip and seemed capable of driving me into the ground if he wanted to.

I answered that I loved Soon-mee and just wanted to see her to tell her that. I don't know how my words sounded to him, but I had to muster all my courage just to say them.

"Love? What love!" the man jeered.

I couldn't bear to have my love scoffed at. "What makes you mock my love for Soon-mee?" I asked him, defiantly.

"This young fellow lacks not only common sense but also prop-er manners. Listen, my sister-in-law says she doesn't know you, ass-hole." It was Soon-mee's elder sister's husband. He had probably rushed over from work after Soon-mee's mother called him. But all this wasn't important to me. I was interested only in Soon-mee, in her words and in her heart.

"That's not true," I shouted. She knows me. *She loves me, she has to, because I love her*, I continued silently to myself. Yes, I was under the delusion that Soon-mee secretly loved me. I knew I shouldn't reveal my love for her because of my brother and I thought she hadn't confessed her love to me for the same reason. So I had to speak out first. Oh, love! Oh, attachment! Oh, what an absurd de-lusion!

"Not true?" the man growled at me. He gave me another scorn-ful smile and then turned around, saying, "Soon-mee, maybe you should talk to this guy."

I turned my head in the same direction that he had. *Had she been here all the while? Had she stood there and watched us? Why didn't she speak up for me?* These questions rushed into my mind. I couldn't believe it, but it was true, there she was. I didn't know how to react. I was happy to see her yet also sad and ashamed for her to find me this way.

"Please say something, Soon-mee," I urged her, feeling miser-able.

But despite my pleading, she passed by without saying a word to me and entered the apartment building. I couldn't tell if she was angry or afraid. Hugging Soon-mee tightly, her mother quickly escorted her away. It reminded me of some dramatic end to a kidnapping scene in a movie, where a mother had just rescued her daughter. I felt wretched. Suddenly, as though I had just awoken from a daydream, I was overwhelmed with terrible self-realization. *Who am I? What am I doing?* Dejected, I collapsed to the ground. Soon-mee's brother-in-law took his hands off me and looked down condescendingly, demonstrating that he was right all along. This gesture was his way of declaring to the spectators who had gathered around us that the situation had been resolved.

"Get lost and never come back. You got off easy today, but I can't guarantee you'll be so lucky next time, understand?" With this warning the man disappeared into the apartment building. The bystanders now scattered and I was left alone. I looked up at Soon-mee's apartment. I could see into the lit living room and there was someone watching me from the window. I thought it might've been Soon-mee. I felt as if I had just been beaten up. The fact that Soon-mee had treated me like a stranger without so much as a word threw me into a bleak state of despair. I rolled over on the ground and began to sob.

11

"You're a piece of garbage!" my brother snarled. "You're not a man, you're a miserable dog." His words were garbled with rage. It was all too impossibly shameful for him to love the same woman that a dog also loved. Yes, it was humiliating for him to accept a situation in which his rival in love was such a total loser. He couldn't even speak, only shriek with anger.

I was on the ground still reeling from Soon-mee's coldheartedness when my brother appeared. I was beginning to totally lose control but my brother took over the situation. Somebody must've contacted him, and it might have been Soon-mee but I was in no position to ask. My brother's face was red and his eyes were aflame. Lifting me up from the ground, he tried again to speak but his words failed to convey any meaning. He brusquely dragged me out of the apartment complex, his grip too powerful for me to even think of escaping. He yanked me up like a dog and pulled me away. I thought that he wanted to kill me—I'm sure the thought crossed his mind.

Finally, he hurled me down onto the grass. We were at a small park located next to the apartment complex. Street lights were lit here and there but it was still quite dark, and since it was late at night no one was about. If he really had the intention of killing me, this wasn't the best place, but it wasn't the worst place either. He threw himself on top of me and began to unleash his anger through his fists. His face was pale with humiliation. It was clear that he didn't really know what to do with me so he just kept punching. I didn't resist, it was a one-sided attack. I didn't believe that I had done anything to deserve such a thrashing. It was blasphemy against my definition of love, which couldn't be influenced by circumstances or social norms. My brother, though, seemed to believe that I had earned a severe beating and so I had to respect his thinking; I couldn't just disregard his belief because it didn't agree with mine. My face soon started bleeding. Blood stained first my clothes and then my brother's. But I didn't feel any pain at all.

"You're . . . trash . . . you're a . . . dog," said my brother, stuttering. "You're an obstacle in my life . . . get lost, please disappear . . . go away," he shouted, before finally beginning to sob. It was him, not me, who was crying. But I wasn't too blind to see how ashamed he was and I wasn't too dumb to realize that having me as a brother is what caused him to feel this way.

I wished he would've just said, clearly and honestly, whatever he felt, such as, "Soon-mee is my girl, so don't even think about her." If he had said that, there could've been some communication between us brothers and I would've been able to explain how I felt deep down. But he didn't want to have such a dialogue with me. His pride probably wouldn't have allowed him to do so. It was simply impossible for him to converse with me, such a worthless piece of trash. I understood him.

Three days later I left home, but it wasn't because my brother had said he wanted me to leave. And I didn't leave because he was violent or because I was afraid of him. I knew there was hardly anything else he could do to me. He could still call me garbage or a dog and, when his anger exploded, he might begin hitting or kicking me again. But what else could he do? When his emotions swelled up uncontrollably he might also start sobbing. I didn't care about his pride; that was something he could only hurt himself with. No, my brother was not the one who drove me away. I left because of Soon-mee. I couldn't forget her coldness toward me. I couldn't escape her face filled with mistrust and misgivings as she blended in with the spectators. I couldn't forget her icy sneer as she walked into the apartment building, her mother hugging her tightly. This scene never left me; it came into my mind whenever I closed my eyes, and it flickered before me like a mirage when my eyes were open. And the reason I hadn't felt any pain while getting thrashed by my brother must've been because her reaction, her indifferent expression, had numbed me. This numbness refused to leave me. It was impossible to live a normal daily life. Time passed and the numbness persisted. I couldn't go on quietly studying for my college entrance exam. I'd lost all the momentum and resolution I'd started out with.

I could no longer stand to live at home with my brother, who was a constant reminder of Soon-mee. But it was my mother who gave me the final impetus to leave home. She acted as if I had done something vile and wicked.

"How could you do such a thing to your brother?" she said. "What did he ever do to you to deserve that?"

I thought she was overreacting. If someone were to have judged me only by my mother's perception, they would have thought I was some sort of violent criminal. And obviously that wasn't the case. I didn't think it was a matter my mother should even get involved in, and if by some chance she happened to be dragged into it, she should have maintained a firm neutrality. But expecting such fairness from her wasn't realistic. I began to detest living at home. Finally, I decided that any other place would be better. Given the situation and that I'd had previous experience living on my own, it was easy for me to leave again.

When I left, I stole my brother's camera, a symbolic act. I did it because I knew that my brother cherished it most among all his belongings. It was much more than just a camera to him. The camera was his vision and voice, more accurate than his eyes and more honest than his words. So without his camera, he wouldn't be able to see or speak. I childishly thought that taking something that he so highly valued would be like taking a piece of his soul. I could only imagine his shock and anger when he noticed that it was gone. I wanted to hurt him as much as possible and thus cut off all my chances of returning home. I used the strategy of a general who eliminated any way of retreating so that only forward movement was possible. And, since I knew the camera was expensive, I also thought it would help me financially now that I was leaving home. Passing through the gate of my house, with the camera bag on my shoulder, I grinned like an ape. The weight of the camera gave me a strange but pleasant tingling sensation which moved along my arm and then spread throughout my whole body.

I took the camera to a store and the proprietor liked it very much. Examining it thoroughly, he asked me, "It's rare to come across a camera like this one. Why do you want to get rid of it?" He couldn't hide his eagerness.

The camera was a Nikon FM2, which my mother had bought for my brother on a trip to Japan. It had been a valuable item at the time, and he later purchased expensive 135 mm and 200 mm lenses for it. The man immediately recognized that it wasn't just an ordinary hobby camera. He didn't suggest a price at first and instead inquired, "Do you have a price in mind?" I took this as his way of being courteous toward a valuable article and its owner. But I wasn't the person the shop owner thought I was, since I had no knowledge of cameras and no love for them either.

Casually, I told him to pay me the best price he could. At that moment he glanced at my face. My expression and tone of voice must have indicated that I was nervous. He seemed to interpret this as my needing to sell the camera because I was in dire straits, regardless of the fact that I loved it as much as my life. As if he understood my feelings very well, he even said unnecessary things, like, "Hmm, it's been well taken care of, I see."

He continued to utter needless remarks, such as telling me that with this model there wasn't much of a price difference between a new and used one. Finally, he made what he said was the best offer he could afford. It was much more than I had imagined. I almost asked him, "It's that expensive?" But I continued to play the part of the sad and resentful photographer who had to sell the camera he loved so dearly due to unexpectedly harsh circumstances. I quickly nodded in agreement to his offer. The proprietor opened his cash register, trying to act like a camera shop owner who empathized with the plight of a photographer in a predicament. Indeed, we were both good actors. The man had been assigned his role and I mine. The world is indeed a stage where we all perform our roles.

Before handing the money to me, the man asked for my name, address, and phone number, a mere formality he said. And I didn't have any reason to decline such an easy thing to do as part of my role. "Sure," I said. I began to write down what he asked for in his account book, but, after a brief hesitation, I gave my brother's name instead of mine. I did so because it didn't seem right to deprive my brother of the ownership of his camera by giving my name; I thought stealing and selling it was bad enough. As if to prove that he was only requesting the information as a mere formality, he didn't confirm my identity and just handed me the money. "Wouldn't you like to make sure the amount is correct?" he asked me. But I shoved the money into my pocket without counting it. "I hope you'll come again. Not many stores here in the Jong-no area have such good merchandise," he added. As I was parting, he smiled solemnly, and in response, I nodded curtly, with a slight frown on my forehead. Yes, to the last moment, we played our roles.

"Wait, there's film in it," the guy yelled out while I was passing through the door.

"It doesn't matter," I replied, without turning my head. I did so as an expression of my indifference. *Why should I have to care about any film left in the camera?* I asked myself. At that moment I couldn't have known that the film in the camera would perform a certain tragic role in our play.

I heard later that the very same week plainclothesmen had raided our home and ransacked my brother's room, confiscating all the photos they found there. The incident caused the arrest of my brother and his friends. The arrest resulted in him being drafted and eventually also cost him his legs. Lastly, it took photography away from him.

Yes, it cost him his legs and photography. He never took any more photos after that. And he lost Soon-mee, too. I don't know the details regarding their parting. All I know is that she isn't with him any longer. I took only his camera, but this action cost him so much more. I have suffered great guilt over the film left in the camera I stole from my brother. The name and address left in the shop owner's account book also brought about the most unfortunate events in my brother's life.

I am a debtor. My debt is huge and heavy. I sometimes feel that the rest of my life will be lived only in order to pay down what I owe my brother.

12

When I showed my brother the new camera, exactly like the one I had sold, he turned his head away without saying a word. He looked as though he had never expected it and as if he didn't fully understand what was happening. Mostly, he looked like he didn't know how to react to me. Studying his face as I carefully weighed my words, I hesitantly told him, "I think you should start taking photos again." Saying this, I felt a sharp pain in my heart for him. I wasn't expecting to redeem myself through this act. I sincerely wished that my brother would recover his old passion for photography. I also hoped that through his camera he might recover his former confidence.

But it hadn't been easy for me to hand the camera over to him. I was ashamed as I knew it would bring up the hurtful, humiliating memories. This is why I had waited for the right time. The camera had sat on my desk for three days like a paperweight, awkward and out of place. And since I knew where it truly belonged, I finally mustered all my courage and went into my brother's room with the camera.

"I rummaged through all the shops in the Jong-no area to find it," I murmured timidly when he didn't respond right away. It was true that I had searched the whole of the Jong-no area. I'd had a substantial amount of cash to spend thanks to my mysterious client who had made another deposit into my account. I wasn't completely comfortable with using the money, especially after I'd shouted at him and said that I wouldn't continue with his case. I should've returned the money to the man but I had no way of doing so and furthermore, he hadn't accepted my refusal. Perhaps my willpower was simply weak. When I'd seen the large sum he had wired into my account, my mind had reeled. I finally decided to keep the cash, not only because my bank account had been low at the time but I had a sense of obligation to help my brother recover his love for photography. The first step toward that goal was to buy him a camera. I tried to convince myself that the money had been given to me for this purpose, which made me feel better about spending it.

I had gone back to the Jong-no area, this time to look for the store where I had sold my brother's camera. I'd thought it would be easy to find, but it wasn't. Stores that all looked alike lined both sides of a narrow street. Each shop had a small sign hanging in front and the names on them were all equally indistinguishable to me. I thought that if I saw the shop owner's face I would recognize him, but this proved impossible since almost every shop owner looked like him: short, balding, and middle-aged with a thick waist and a red face. Finally, after a long while meandering through the streets in search of the store, I asked myself whether locating the exact store was really necessary. I changed my plan and stopped to rest my legs. Even if I could have found the exact store that I'd sold my brother's camera to years before, his camera probably wouldn't be there now. It would've been perfect and touching if I had been able to recover his camera, which he had given not only his time but also his soul. But it was absurd to expect that it would still be there so I finally concluded that a camera that was the exact same model as his would be good enough. I randomly entered one of the many camera shops and bought a Nikon FM2. It cost quite a bit of money.

Sputtering and stumbling as I spoke, I told my brother the whole story as he sat in uncomfortable silence. "What a waste," he finally said. Clearly, he was uninterested in my suggestion. I pretended not to understand him but I was determined to at least try to convince him. I faltered at first but then began to speak and the thoughts I had planned to express unwound effortlessly.

"Do you remember? I used to go into your room to look at your photos. And sometimes you explained them to me. Excitedly, you would point out the truth in the photos. 'This is truth,' you would say. And when you said, 'I take photos to capture the truth, to communicate the truth, and to prove the truth,' you looked powerful and dignified. I learned the truths of our times through your photos. I didn't read newspapers; I didn't need to, because nothing was more honest than your photos. I saw the raw truth in them. Through your photos I learned of the sadness and despair of our reality and I saw its anger and tears." My solemn voice seemed to fill the room. I hadn't intended to be so serious but the tone of my words was heavy. I wonder why some memories can never be brought up lightly even as time passes. "But . . . I've . . . always felt that something was missing from your photos," I continued. "At first I didn't know what it was, but I thought that maybe shooting some flowers, trees, clouds, or ocean scenes would be a nice change. I always wished that your photos could record not only the weight of truth but also the softness of beauty. I generally agreed with your view of photography, but sometimes I wished that you would go beyond your moral angle and your ethical focus to see things from an empathetic angle or an imaginative focus. I wished that your strong belief in photography's capacity to capture the truth in history and society could open you up to other values, freer and lighter, like the beauty in nature and in people. I wished that you could've captured truth's other faces, like a nude woman, or a person you love, or the beauty of nature. As you must remember, I secretly went into your room and rummaged through your things, right? Those times I think I was also looking to see if your photos ever captured other truths such as beauty and love."

At this last statement my brother frowned. *Don't try to return to the past!* I knew then that I should've stopped talking, but I couldn't. An uncontrollable urge propelled me to continue. "Please, pick up the camera. Look at the world through it. You should let your camera capture the beauty of the world. I would then feel that I was a tiny bit forgiven. Do it for me, please."

I'd said too much and now I could tell my brother had been agitated by my words. I saw his pupils lose focus, as if they were floating in the white of his eyes, before they vanished under his eyelids. His complexion became so pale it looked like clear plastic film and his face distorted like a crumpled wad of paper. He twisted his body in an attempt to control his violent impulses. His mouth opened wide, like he was preparing for choir practice, and a slow scream erupted from him. It was the sound of an animal. As if he couldn't bear the heat radiating from his body, he grabbed his T-shirt and violently pulled it down away from his throat. The thin cotton was soon ripped apart. Not satisfied with this, he now tore the parts into smaller and smaller pieces. When most of his clothes had been torn away, he then began scratching his body. He stuck his fingernails into his soft white flesh which had not been exposed to the sun for so long. Soon red lines crisscrossed his chest as he scratched himself repeatedly. He then rolled about on the floor as if he was on fire, slamming his head against the floor and walls. He was sweating and bleeding, his face bruised. And he continued shrieking, monstrously. Yes, a monster living inside him was writhing and struggling to escape from his body.

Bewildered, I didn't know what to do. At first I just watched him. And when I had finally collected myself, I didn't have the strength to hold him down. I was shocked to see that this destructive power had been hibernating inside him. It was as if an explosive had been hidden in his body, and it had now detonated. Maybe it would be more accurate to say his body itself was the explosive. My mother had once said "He's usually okay, but when he has a fit, he tears his clothes, claws at his body until it's all black and blue, and bangs his head against things . . . it couldn't be worse." I saw now that her words were true, his actions now proved it. I then remembered that she also said something else: "He then takes off his clothes and crawls all over the house, doing terrible things. I'm sorry to say it, but . . . he masturbates, spraying his sperm everywhere . . . it's just unbearable." Unbearable. Remembering this word, I felt as if my windpipe was blocked and I couldn't breathe. Unbearable! With my eyes closed, I grabbed my brother. He continued writhing, naked, and his face, smeared with his own blood and sweat, was ghastly to look at. My face and clothes were also soiled with his blood and sweat, and try as I might, I just couldn't match his strength.

Who's home now? I wondered. The maid had gone grocery shopping. I finally kicked the door open and shouted, "Is there anybody here? Please, help me . . . come quick . . . please help me!"

My father, who I knew was home, didn't appear immediately. My brother had torn off all of his clothes and was crawling about on the floor completely naked, uttering sounds that were neither cries nor laughter when my father finally appeared. Seeing him standing in the doorway, I motioned toward my brother, pleading for my father to do something. He had heard everything and knew what was happening and he didn't look at all surprised. Instead, he stared at my brother impassively and then simply said to me, "Leave him alone."

Leave him alone? I didn't understand how my father could say that. "Look at him. Don't you see how much he's suffering? How can you say to leave him alone? How?" I asked, baffled.

But Father only repeated what he had just said, only much more sternly: "Leave him alone and get out of the room." It was the sternest voice I had ever heard him use, and I had no other choice but to obey. Leaving my brother, who was now violently jerking his hand up and down on his erection, Father and I exited the room. As he left, my father slammed the door with a bang.

"Miserable fellow!" my father spat, going into his own room. But I didn't know who he was referring to, me, or my brother.

My brother's fit lasted for thirty minutes. And my father knew that he should be left alone when he's in that state. It would only make things worse if anyone tried to do anything while it was happening.

It looked as if a bomb had exploded in my brother's room after his outburst. His things were broken, smashed, and torn. And like just another of the shattered objects strewn across the floor, my brother's naked body was sprawled among the destruction. His eyes were closed, his limbs limp. The sight of his legs, cut off right below the knees, pierced my heart. His bruised body was evidence of his struggle. His room was also filled with a sour smell. His sperm covered the floor and wall and some of his things. Attempting to find a place to stand on the slippery floor, I looked around, distraught. Incompatible emotions, such as compassion and disgust, sadness and anger, tangled up inside hindering my movement.

"Step aside," my father said, entering my brother's room and nudging me out of his way. Inside the room Father let out a deep sigh and opened the window, muttering under his breath before picking up my brother, still sprawled out on the floor, and carrying him to the bathroom. My brother had regained consciousness and allowed himself to be lifted up like a baby.

Father sat my brother in a chair in the bathtub that had been custom designed for him and turned on the water. He adjusted the temperature before aiming the showerhead at my brother. Although he remained still under the stream of water, his eyes and mouth were sealed so tightly that it seemed he was desperately battling against some violent upheaval. His face was fully charged with emotions that were ready to burst out again at a moment's notice. I couldn't bear to look at his face so I returned to his room and began cleaning up. My movements were stiff and slow, as I tried to avoid the sticky puddles on the floor.

Father carefully soaped and rinsed my brother and then dried him with a towel. In contrast to my awkward motions, my father's every move was meticulous and concise. It was unusual to see him like this. I wondered what he was thinking, but I didn't ask.

He put my brother on his bed. His naked body reminded me of a baby's. It looked to me that my brother had now entered the innocent world of a child, where no lust or shame existed. Father put some ointment on my brother's scratches and then covered him with a thin blanket. Father did all this in silence. I saw my brother pulling the blanket up to cover his head as he turned toward the wall. Watching him, I felt unidentifiable emotions rise up inside me.

Father then wet a rag and began cleaning my brother's room. "I can do it," I said, but I didn't take the rag from his hand. Knowing that I was just trying to be polite, he didn't even reply as he continued cleaning. Father threw out the damaged things and went back and forth into the bathroom to wash his rag. To the last moment, he remained calm. My brother's body heaved up and down as he sobbed under the blanket. Feeling awkward standing there and just watching it all, I finally left the room.

13

I was filled with turbulent emotions after having finally witnessed one of my brother's violent outbursts. I felt like I couldn't breathe and I needed to get some fresh air so I decided to return to the forest path at the site of the royal tomb, where I had seen the pine tree entwined with the slick snowbell and where I had finally faced the dark forest, so far removed from any human footsteps. I remembered my brother's sobbing, his face sunk in darkness, and, all of a sudden, I had the realization that Soon-mee was still embedded in the deepest part of his heart. Psychiatrists say that the first step in healing a psychological problem is facing the root of the issue. If that was true then the only person who could heal my brother was Soon-mee, not some woman at the Lotus Flower Market. The truth seemed so obvious, I must have known it all along but I didn't want to admit it. Even though I was dying to know, I hadn't tried to find out how my brother and Soon-mee had parted, where she was living now, or what she was doing. This was because she still remained embedded in my heart as well. I was afraid of reawakening my old obsession by entering her reality or letting her enter mine. It would be too much for me. If I had been able to forget her, it would've been a totally different matter. But I didn't want to forget her. I believed it would be enough to let her carry on her life somewhere else. I had left home as a way to test whether I could live in a world where she didn't exist, and I had passed this test—but not completely. So when I returned home I was glad that she wasn't with my brother any longer. But sometimes the sound of her singing and guitar playing would spring vividly to mind. At those times, as before, I let myself imagine that she sang only for me, though I would quickly feel embarrassed by my ridiculous thoughts. Soon-mee no longer existed in my world, and

I felt that was how it should be. But now my conscience was tell-ing me that I had to find her. It was more like an impulse than a logical conclusion, but I held the firm belief that impulse often re-vealed the divine. Reuniting my brother and Soon-mee weighed on me like an important mission that I had to complete. Even though I had no plan as to what I would do once I found her, I felt that I couldn't postpone it any longer. With this strange sudden urge, I hastily walked down the forest path and back home.

As I neared our house I thought about what my next step should be. I figured that my brother would have needed a long nap after his exhausting fit and even if he was now awake, it wouldn't be the right time to ask him about Soon-mee. I could ask my fa-ther, but I wasn't sure if he knew anything. I wanted to speak with him about how he had taken care of my brother; it was so out of character for him and it had been touching to see. I realized that I didn't know my father very well and I soon asked myself how much I knew about my mother and brother. I quickly came to the con-clusion that I knew next to nothing about anyone in my family. We shared some space and a little time together, that's all; it was sad. Like surging water, this sadness washed over me and, as if in an attempt to reach higher ground, I started running home at full speed.

Father was watching TV. When he wasn't playing baduk alone, watering the plants, or out on a walk, he would undoubtedly be sitting in front of the TV set. Our television service had a twenty-four hour broadcast and over fifty channels. Father, though, didn't flip around to different channels. His TV was always on the Ba-duk Channel. He didn't watch any news or dramas at all. And he didn't read newspapers; it just wasn't like him. He seemed not to care what was happening in the world.

Father looked a bit tired. And he acted as if he hadn't even seen me enter his room with some coffee for him. I put the coffee down in front of him and looked at what he was watching on TV. A busi-nessman was faced off against a professional ba-duk player. Judg-ing by the caption on the screen he was challenging a level three player, and if he defeated him he would become a level three player himself. Father glared at the screen. Father was concentrated on the screen testing his skill against the players on TV. But it was boring for someone like me who didn't know much about the game. Nonetheless, I sat next to my father and watched as I drank my coffee. Seemingly unaware of the fact that I was sitting next to him, he kept his eyes on the tedious game and left his coffee untouched. I knew that I needed to wait for the game to end in order to speak to him, but I had no idea when it would end. I finished my coffee and left the room with my empty cup.

I went into my room, opened the inside pocket of my travel bag, and took out Soon-mee's tape. I hadn't listened to it in such a long time. It was one of the few things I had taken, along with my brother's camera, when I'd left home. While I'd been away I had listened to the tape whenever Soon-mee crossed my mind. You see, like I said, I never felt that I had to forget her and I didn't even try to forget her. So there wasn't any reason for me not to listen to her songs. Actually, listening to her songs, again and again, had seemed to soothe the pain I'd felt over Soon-mee's rejection. If I hadn't had the tape, I probably would've sought her out numerous times. But since returning home, I hadn't even taken the tape out of my travel bag. I hadn't listened to it out of respect for my brother, and, at the same time, because I was now able to manage my emotions without listening to her songs. This was one of the reasons I had decided I could return home.

I placed the tape in the cassette player and put on my headphones. Old habits are hard to shake; I still didn't want to share her songs with anyone. "I gave my heart to you. But here I've stood for such a long time without even a glance from you. How much longer will I stand here waiting for you? Before I melt away, before I melt away, like snow without a trace, take my heart, my photographer . . ." Her voice seeped into my body like some kind of perfume. Indeed, the old me was all too easily awakened by thoughts of Soon-mee.

14

It wasn't that difficult to find Soon-mee, as this was the kind of task I was used to. I remembered the apartment where her family had lived years before. And I also had her old address and phone number. And so I called her. When I said that I was looking for Soon-mee, an old woman with a hoarse voice bluntly replied that no woman with such a name lived there and then abruptly hung up. So I called the operator and got Soon-mee's new number.

From the administrator's office at her old apartment complex, I discovered that Soon-mee's family had moved away three years before. But her family's new home was still in Seoul and wasn't that far away. I called her new number. A thick-voiced man whom I assumed to be Soon-mee's father answered. As soon as I told him I was looking for her, he asked me who I was. Not knowing what to say, I hesitated momentarily. *Who am I to her?* I asked myself. But the more important question at that moment was who he thought I was. I sensed some mistrust in his voice when he said, "Looking for Soon-mee?" Embarrassed and not really sure what to say, I told him that I was an old friend of hers. But he still didn't seem to trust me and he didn't even ask for my name before hanging up, saying, "Soon-mee isn't here."

I was certain that she no longer lived with her parents so I didn't think I needed to call again. She must have left home by now, either to live on her own or she might have gotten married. Neither option would have been strange or unexpected. After all, she was already thirty. Still, I couldn't help feeling a sense of disappointment at the fact that whatever had become of her, she would never be mine.

The following morning I decided to call her parents again to ask for her new phone number. The man who I'd thought was Soon-mee's father didn't recognize my voice. This was because he had never received a phone call from the president of Soon-mee's college alumni association. This was a trick I had learned at The Runners. When I said that the school's alumni association was setting up a reunion for all the graduates and I wanted to confirm Soon-mee's contact information, her father readily gave me her new address and phone number. I thanked him and hung up.

She had moved to a small city located east of Seoul. She had a flat in a five-story apartment building on a hillside. I had plenty of time to admire the tall trees with wide leaves that shaded the complex as I hid out across from her building for seventeen hours. Seventeen hours is a long time but I'd been through worse. Once, when I was working for The Runners, I had waited in one spot for twenty-eight hours. I was investigating a woman who took that long to come out of her house. The client was her husband who believed his wife was having an affair.

This time my hideout was on the rooftop of a commercial building. From there I had a full view of Soon-mee's flat across the street, including her front door. Throughout the whole afternoon her window curtains were drawn. When the sun set and the street lights were lit the curtains opened. By then I had finished my third can of coffee. And while opening a fourth, I saw her living room light up. All the memories I had of her, a short bob hairstyle, no makeup, white T-shirt, and laughter as fresh as spring sunshine, were still vivid, and when I saw all this again through my binoculars, I gasped, as if something had knocked the wind out of me. She was exactly the same even down to the short hair and no makeup.

Soon-mee walked around her living room lightly; it was as if she were floating in midair. She soon went into her bedroom and came out wearing different clothes. The sky-blue dress she changed into had a Disney cartoon character printed on it. She looked like a slender, supple fish swimming around in the room. She entered the bathroom next and soon came out wiping her face with a towel. Afterwards, in the kitchen, she put her groceries into the refrigerator, turned on the water, washed a peach, and took a big bite out of it. I imagined the peach juice streaming down through her fingers.

She then began to prepare dinner: she trimmed, washed, cut, and boiled her food while repeatedly opening and closing the refrigerator. When she was done cooking, she sat on the sofa and turned on the TV with her remote control but soon turned it off and switched on her stereo system instead. Of course I couldn't hear which CD she played; I could only see her movement. She leaned her head back and rested it comfortably against the sofa, which was upholstered in a blue fabric with geometric patterns on it. She stayed in that position for a long time. And I watched every single move she made through my binoculars. She seemed to have her eyes closed and she seemed tired. After some time had passed, I thought maybe she had fallen asleep.

Putting down the binoculars, I looked around for more coffee, but there was none left. Crushing the empty can, I decided I had to call her. Taking out my cell phone, I dialed her number. The phone rang. Looking through the binoculars, I kept focused on her living room. I didn't want to miss one single move. I wished I could see the breath she was breathing in and out and I longed to hear the music she was listening to. The phone rang a second time. And she finally moved. She lifted her head up from the sofa and then turned around. At the third ring she slowly raised her body, and I saw that she walked less nimbly, as if she was still half asleep. My heart swelled. *Now she'll answer the phone*, I thought to myself. I covered my cell phone with my palm to block the sound of my panting as I tried to catch my breath. The phone rang twice more and then Soon-mee disappeared from sight. She appeared again immediately but she wasn't alone. She had exited the stage for a moment only to reappear with a man in a brown suit, another character. The man flung his black briefcase onto the sofa and then sat himself down where Soon-mee had just rested. Loosening his necktie, he said something, but of course I couldn't hear it. All the while, the phone continued to ring until Soon-mee finally walked hastily toward it, as if she felt sorry for the caller, but wished the phone would stop ringing. She was still talking with the man when she picked up the receiver. I finally heard her voice.

"Hello?" she said.

But I was unable to speak. The distance between my turbulent emotional state and her nonchalant way of answering the phone was disconcerting. *I can't talk to her while I'm watching her like this,* I said to myself. *No, it isn't right to talk to her on the phone while I spy on her. Even if video-phones become popular, I'll never use them.* These random thoughts jumbled up in my mind.

"Hello? Who's calling, please?" she asked.

She urged me to respond but I couldn't. She shrugged her shoulders at the man on the sofa and he did the same. I heard his voice in the background but couldn't make it out. The man then made a gesture that I couldn't easily interpret through the binoculars but he seemed to want her to hang up the phone and come into his arms. She put the receiver down and walked over to him. My eyes were still glued to the lenses of my binoculars. *No, it's not right to talk on the phone with someone while spying on them,* I said again to myself. Soon-mee sat on the man's lap. Like vines wrapping around a tree trunk, his arms encircled her. I watched her snuggle up to him. And I watched his hands roam sensually all over her body.

Distraught, I accidently dropped my binoculars. Hitting the cement, one of the lenses cracked. I wasn't able to continue spying on them. I slumped down to the ground and sat there for quite a while, slow to recover my composure. And in my self-pity I let out a bitter laugh. *Who am I to Soon-mee?* I asked myself. I was the person who listened to her songs secretly. The person whose heart burst with love while listening to the songs she sang for someone else. I was the person who was once again spying on her after all this time while she was again with another man and not me. I felt terrible. I knew it was absurd but I had the feeling that she was doing all this to purposely humiliate me.

Losing sight of why I had even gone there in the first place, I commanded myself to leave. *Leave her now!* My survival instinct didn't want to revive the humiliating past. I stood up and saw that they were now sitting at the table. I couldn't make out the details without my binoculars, but imagined them happily eating dinner together. Turning around, I quickly scurried down from the roof of the building.

15

She left her apartment at 8:20 the following morning. Her car was dark red. I had parked my car in front of her building to wait for her. She drove slowly. It was easy to follow her at a safe distance.

The previous night I had been unable to leave the area. I had reminded myself that my brother's wellbeing, not my own feelings, had compelled me to search for Soon-mee. But perhaps my lingering attachment to her had kept me there as well. I had considered getting a bite to eat but instead I went into a nearby bar and had some beers before slowly stumbling, like a drunkard, back toward the spot in front of her apartment building. Still upset, I bought some more beer before going back up to the roof.

Like a stage after the play has ended, her apartment was dark and the curtains were drawn. I've always been curious about what actors and actresses do backstage once the play ends. Expecting to maybe see something, I used to stare at the curtains after a play had ended. And now once more I opened my eyes wide and this time gazed at the movements I perceived behind Soon-mee's curtains. I couldn't make out what was going on and when I used my imagination my heart began to beat fast and I became giddy. I was reminded of the times when I used to secretly sneak into my brother's room. *She belongs to another man, then and now . . .* I said to myself—and it was the truth.

Alone on the cement rooftop, still warm from the day's sun, I sat drinking beer. If the guard hadn't appeared and aimed his flashlight at me, I would've stayed there until the following morning.

"What are you doing here?" he shouted from the doorway. His flashlight shot a beam of light at me. I raised my hand to block it. "Sir, no one's allowed to loiter here," he said without coming closer. He must've been either cowardly or cautious. I raised my hand again, this time to signal that I understood what he had said, and I then promptly stood up. Empty beer cans were scattered all around me. To vent my misery, I kicked them away.

Before leaving, I glanced at her apartment, but the curtains were still drawn. I asked the guard what time it was. Looking closely at his face, I saw that he was quite old and wrinkled. "It's about 11:00," he answered, still looking at me suspiciously. I walked past him and down the steps.

I thought of just going home. Soon-mee looked happy with the man who was no doubt her husband. *Why do I have to reopen old wounds that have now healed? I'm not sure what it would do to my brother and to me, but I know it wouldn't be any good for her . . .* I think I really would've left if, and only if, I hadn't met the man downstairs leaving her apartment building. Wearing his brown suit and with his black briefcase in hand, he walked toward me. He looked exactly the same as he had when he entered Soon-mee's apartment. He passed very close as he strode toward his car. I studied his face when he passed and fortunately streetlights were lit here and there so it was bright enough for me to satisfy my curiosity. The man's short hair was neat and tidy, and he wore glasses over his piercing eyes. He had a reddish complexion.

Confidently, his back straight, he moved away from me as I continued to stare. I had the feeling that the man was familiar. This vague sensation persisted and I stood motionless, trying to remember where I had seen him before. A faint memory flashed into my mind and then vanished. The man's car, the same color as his suit, sped away. Something about the man made me suspicious and my heart throbbed at the thought of Soon-mee being alone all night—to be honest, it excited me. I calmed myself down and turned to the issue of the man in the brown suit. *Where have I seen that guy before?*

When the lights of Soon-mee's apartment went out I decided to stay the night at a nearby motel. It must've been my drinking that had made me so drowsy. An unfounded hope that everything would be okay after I had some sleep got me into bed. I soon fell into a shallow sleep, punctuated by many dreams. Meandering through them, I was awoken by a startling realization. I sat up in bed. "That bastard!" I uttered. And after that, I was unable to go back to sleep. I waited for dawn and then left the motel in the still lingering darkness.

After tailing Soon-mee for a while, I had reached the municipal library. I parked my car some distance away and mulled the situation over. Something about the way she had walked inside suggested that she wasn't a mere visitor to the library. I assumed that she worked there, and this assumption soon proved correct. Since the library opened at nine, I waited outside for about thirty minutes and then walked in to see Soon-mee sitting behind the circulation desk. Leaning against a bookshelf, I watched as she studied the computer monitor, her head slightly bent.

Her short hair was cut in the same style and she wore no makeup. And she still had an unusually fair complexion. But her face was no longer filled with laughter, laughter as bright as spring sunshine. Her profile reminded me of a tree's leaf in the shade. And I concluded that this change was simply a sign of time passing.

Industrious people were already entering the library at that early hour, idly sitting or standing as they flipped through their books, but the place wasn't exactly busy. I wished Soon-mee would look up and spot me, but she never even lifted her head. When people had selected books and brought them to her, she checked them out, keeping her head down all the while. I had the impression that for some reason she was avoiding people's faces. It seemed as if some disquieting thought lurked in her mind. Just then, like lightening, the brown-suited man's face flashed again across my mind's eye. It was the same face that had mockingly spit out the word "Love?" ridiculing me, as if it were laughable. His derision of my love for Soon-mee had been humiliating. Many years had passed but the moment was as vivid in my memory as if it had happened only yesterday.

Soon-mee got up and walked toward the bookshelves. She passed right in front of me with an armful of books. The books, stacked up to her chin, looked unstable. As she walked by, the air stirred up and I inhaled deeply to catch her scent. She smelled like peaches. She didn't see me as she walked with her head back, trying to hold the books steady between her arms and chin. I wondered whether she would even recognize me if she saw me.

Soon-mee had barely taken a few steps past me when she tripped. The tall stack of books wobbled and as she lost her balance they tumbled down and scattered all over the floor. Some books traveled quite a distance. "Oh, my!" she cried out. It was as if she had called out to me alone. I confidently walked toward her, forgetting all my previous doubts and reservations. Bending down, she began to gather up the books, one by one. From the same bent position, I helped her collect them.

"Thank you," she said, in a barely audible voice. I stacked the books back up on her arms.

"Can I help you?" I asked. My voice was shaking.

"It's okay, but thanks," she answered, pressing the pile of books down with her chin. I became impatient and agitated. I wished that she would raise her head and look at my face. I wanted to see her expression when she recognized me. But, as if she had indeed decided not to look at people's faces, she kept her gaze down. I blocked her path, refusing to step aside to make room for her.

"It's okay," she said once more, indicating that she wanted me to move. I ignored this and just stood there. Finally, she lifted her head to look at the person who was barring her way.

For a moment Soon-mee's face, which before had resembled a shaded leaf, now reflected disbelief and then total shock. With her mouth agape, she let out a short "Oh, my." With this, the books in her arms again fell to the floor. Bending down, I picked the books back up. Her eyes anxiously searched around. Her reaction clearly revealed her alarm and fear of me. And this made me sad. Of course, I hadn't hoped for a warm welcome from her, but still, this wasn't what I'd expected either.

I felt terrible but I somehow managed to say in a composed voice, "Don't be alarmed." I said it in a comforting tone, as if I were consoling a person in shock. In response, she dropped her gaze back down to the floor. Her reaction unnerved me, so I hastily told her that I had come to ask her a favor. "I don't want to talk about myself. It's not about me. Don't worry," I quickly said. My voice was pleading as though I were desperately trying to win her favor or attention. My words were sincere. At that moment I was only there to play the role of the younger brother who had to see her for the sake of his older brother. I saw Soon-mee shake her head a couple of times, and she quickly collected herself. Then she walked away between the bookshelves. I followed her.

I stood behind her and began to speak as she began to stack books. "I came to this area yesterday. I didn't know that you worked at the library. It fits you, the work, I mean. I've been watching you . . . it feels strange."

I didn't tell her that I had spied on her the previous night. And, of course, I didn't mention anything about the man in the brown suit. "I have something to tell you. And again, it's not about me. Believe me, I won't talk about myself. Actually, I don't have much to say about me. You don't have any interest in my story, anyway. But listen, do you know how my brother is doing now? That's what I want to ask you first. The next thing I want to know is why you two broke up. Did you leave him because he became what he is now? I'm not blaming you for that. I was a little sad about your leaving, but it's surely understandable. It actually hasn't been that long since I returned home and found out about him. He's now in serious condition. It's very bad. And coming to you was my idea— I think you can help him. That's why I came here today. That's why I had to find you."

Soon-mee, who had been silently arranging books on the shelves, suddenly froze. "Are you saying that something has happened to Woo-hyeon?"

16

"What happened to him?" Soon-mee asked me. I was surprised to discover that she knew nothing about my brother. She didn't know that he had lost his legs and often had wild fits, and, of course, she didn't know about his regular trips to the Lotus Flower Market or now to motels on the outskirts of Seoul for the same purpose. As she kept asking me questions, I kept answering them. She had difficulty believing what I said about my brother, asking the same questions, over and over again, shaking her head like she wanted to deny it all. In the stacks, a forest filled with the familiar moldy smell of books, she and I had a long conversation. Now and then people passed by in search of books, but they didn't pay any attention to us. The library was quiet in the morning. As we talked, Soon-mee sometimes hid her face behind a book, as if to conceal her reactions to what I was saying. She also occasionally leaned against a bookshelf, placing more than half her weight against it. I worried that she might faint. Finally, she squatted down. Burying her face in her palms, she placed her head on her knees. She was trying to hide her tears from me.

"I . . . didn't know," she said. I didn't say anything to suggest I didn't believe her, but she again said, "It's true, I really didn't know." She paused for a moment. "At first, but not that often, he mailed me letters when he was in the military, but they suddenly stopped. And he no longer responded to my letters after that. So relying on the address that I had, I took a trip to where he was stationed. A tall MP, with sergeant markings on his uniform, was standing guard at the gate, and he told me that your brother had transferred to a different base. I asked him why and he said such things often happen in the military. I then asked him where his new camp was and he said he didn't know." Soon-mee was almost in tears. She looked as if she were confessing all her sins. And this attitude made me uncomfortable, since as far as I knew, she was blameless. "Do you think the guard lied to me?" she asked, in a trembling voice.

As a person unfamiliar with military regulations or practices, I couldn't answer her. Instead, I asked "Didn't you contact my family?"

"Of course I did. And your mother said that he was out of the country," she immediately answered.

I was confused. I had no idea what my mother could have been referring to. Soon-mee said that she had asked her for an explanation. And my mother answered that my brother had left the military a year before his scheduled discharge date due to a health issue and that he had gone to America for treatment. Soon-mee then naturally asked what the health problem was and mother answered that he had a lump in his lymph node. Mother also told her that it was a kind of cancer but not that serious. When Soon-mee asked her how he was doing, Mother said that his surgery was successful and he was recovering.

"And did you believe all that?" I asked her, revealing my doubts about what she had just said.

"There was no reason not to believe her," she answered, as if I should be ashamed to doubt her. "There was nothing to do but to believe what your mother said, and so I was mainly concerned about his health . . . until . . ." she stopped short, absently flipping through an old book with thick covers. She eventually became suspicious about what my mother had told her, and I wondered what had made her begin to doubt. "I asked your mother when Woo-hyeon would come back home. I thought that since his surgery had been successful and his recuperation was going well, he would be back soon. And, of course, I missed him a lot. But your mother told me that he wouldn't be returning. Her answer really surprised me, and so I asked, 'What do you mean by that?' We had met at a coffee shop alongside a river, but she didn't even touch her coffee and it got cold. I also remember her face then . . . she looked distraught and unusually sad. And all the while, she let out heavy sighs that seemed to reflect her emotions. I don't know why I was so dumb and so totally oblivious to the possibility that something terrible had happened to Woo-hyeon. After another heavy sigh, your mother told me that he would remain abroad at his uncle's home and would continue his studies there. It was such unexpected news that I really didn't know how to respond to it. And as you now know, I hadn't directly heard anything from your brother. So I think it was then that I finally felt something was wrong. Your mother stopped speaking, too. For quite some time we remained silent. After a long while, I told her that I wanted to call your brother, and I said this not because I couldn't bear the stifling silence any longer but because I finally detected something suspicious in your mother's face and manner. 'No, don't call him,' she immediately said, and her hand was signaling a firm rejection. She didn't look directly at me when she did this, but her response was as strong as a smack across my face. Even a dimwit couldn't have missed the meaning of such a response. It was a clear and stern refusal. I interpreted it as, 'No, don't you dare.' I was so embarrassed that I couldn't even ask her why. It was very difficult for me to accept all this," Soon-mee concluded.

"I understand," I told her, fixing my gaze at her fair face. Her long eyelashes were fluttering and she once again looked like an exotic plant from a land of shadows.

"I didn't get any letters or phone calls from your brother. I was so anxious about him that I was losing my patience. Finally, I couldn't wait any longer, so I contacted your mother again, but she said that she had told me what she could and that she didn't need to see me, since there wasn't any reason for it. I was taken aback by her coldness. And . . ." Soon-mee stopped suddenly. She brushed her hair aside and then remained silent for a while, not wanting to finish what she was about to say. I saw that her eyelashes were again quivering slightly, as if she was holding back tears. I said nothing, silently letting her know that I was waiting for her to speak. "I asked someone to find out what was really going on with your brother. I wanted to know whether your mother had told me the truth or not and whether Woo-hyeon wanted to leave me, and, if so, what the reason was. By then I was so beside myself. During that time I only thought of him, nothing else, and I became paranoid. Luckily, I had someone close to me working at the National Intelligence Agency and so I asked him to find out about your brother." With this, Soon-mee stopped speaking again.

It must've been difficult for her to recall such a painful time from her past. I sensed her reluctance to trust me but it wasn't the right time to talk about myself. So I asked her whether she now understood the situation: my mother must have hidden the truth about my brother because my brother didn't want her to know about his physical condition and he had convinced my mother to lie.

"No, I really don't understand. That's not what I heard," she said, frowning with confusion. "The information that the Intelligence Agency collected about Woo-hyeon confirmed everything your mother had told me. It was true that Woo-hyeon went abroad to have surgery done on his lymph gland and that he stayed at a relative's house in America and was studying there. But in addition to all this, I discovered more shocking news. He was engaged to the daughter of a wealthy man who owned a medical center! And I heard that she was a student at the same school he attended and that they would soon be married in America. I was also told that he would never come back to me and that I shouldn't harbor any hope about this. So . . . what was I supposed to do after finding all this out? Or what do you think I should've done?" Her voice was heavy with emotion. She looked too weak to stand on her own and I saw her hands tighten around the edge of the bookshelf. But I couldn't stretch out an arm to steady her; I just couldn't bridge the distance between us. Her hands released their grip and she dropped to the floor, where she squatted down and curled her body in on itself.

"Are you okay?" I asked her.

"I'm fine," she answered.

"I don't understand why someone would have told you those lies," I said. "My brother never left for a foreign country to study nor was he ever engaged, as far as I know. If it were true, I would've known."

She seemed to agree with me. "It's a puzzle to me too. What's going on?" she asked, as if to herself. She looked like she was searching her memory to make rational sense of it all. I did the same. I went back to the past and tried to put things together coherently. But I got lost in the maze of lies. I could understand why my mother had lied to Soon-mee, but why would the person at the Intelligence Agency feel the need to lie? The ideas in my head were jumbled up beyond comprehension.

"Could you tell me who the investigator was?" I asked. "They must've had some good reason for making up all those lies." I was suspicious. Everything was still quite murky but I had an idea.

"Well, maybe . . ." she stopped short, evading my question.

"I'm just guessing, but was the person at the Intelligence Agency your elder sister's husband?" I asked. I felt like a shrewd detective following a hunch. For the first time Soon-mee lifted her head and looked directly at me. She appeared both embarrassed and surprised by my question. It seemed that my instinct had been correct, which made me giddy but I had to be careful not to hurt her feelings. I avoided her eyes. She covered her face with her hands and rested her head against her knees. Her shoulders shook as her pent-up emotions were finally being released. I couldn't just come out and tell her that I had seen her brother-in-law at her apartment the previous night. And I certainly couldn't interrogate her about what the man had been doing there, even though I was eager to know.

"I need some time alone to think," she said, still squatting on the floor between the bookshelves. Her voice revealed her struggle to make some sense of the situation. I wanted to put my hand on her curled back. I wanted to pat her shoulders and tell her gently not to worry, that life isn't as overwhelming as we sometimes think but it isn't as predictable as we often expect; some days are overcast and some days it rains but the sun is always up in the sky and that's life. But I couldn't comfort her. My brother's face appeared in my mind, stopping me cold. Consumed by emotions, Soon-mee began to sob. I stood there motionless watching her shoulders tremble.

Before leaving the library I told Soon-mee that I was trying to convince my brother to take up photography again. "Please help my brother to begin again," I said. She looked at me, her eyes filled with tears.

17

When my mother asked me to purchase a roundtrip train ticket for a three-day trip she said she had to take, I wondered if she already knew that I was following her for a mysterious client and was slyly testing me to see how I would react to her request. Maybe I was paranoid because she asked me to do this immediately after I'd had another loud telephone argument with the client. He'd called me on my cell phone asking for a progress report on my mother and I'd shouted that I wouldn't reveal any information until he identified himself and his purpose. I'd meant what I'd said but I still couldn't drop the case. Keeping the case meant I didn't have to feel guilty about tailing my own mother, which I continued to do mainly out of curiosity. But I also felt obligated to protect my mother from any possible danger. I decided that the fact this case had been handed to me of all people was a stroke of luck. If someone else had been investigating her, then she wouldn't be protected at all.

For some reason Mother looked sad when she asked me to get the train ticket for her. She asked where I had been but I didn't tell her that I had gone to see Soon-mee. I wanted to confront my mother about what Soon-mee had said but I wasn't sure if it was a wise thing to do. I scratched my head and ignored her question, and Mother, who really didn't seem that interested in my whereabouts, instead started talking about her trip. "I need you to take care of a roundtrip ticket to Namcheon, departing tomorrow morning. How much do you charge for this service?" Awkwardly, I grinned and she did too. She then handed me an amount that would have been enough to buy plane tickets and said the rest was for my service.

"Why don't you drive?" I asked. She said it would be too long of a drive for her. "Well, maybe I can drive. How about that?" I said, casually. Driving her to Namcheon myself would be perfect, both for spying on her and protecting her.

She gave my offer some thought but soon said, "Thank you, but it's not necessary; I really want to travel by train."

I bought the ticket Mother needed and rented a car with the rest of the money. Almost as if she had known I would do exactly that, the money left over after purchasing her ticket was just enough to rent a car. Of course, I had some reservations about following her, but I had already decided to do so when she told me she was leaving town. It was my job so I had to do it even though I suspected Mother might already know all about my case. I was naturally quite curious about her trip, especially since my family had no connection to Namcheon. I had this unshakeable thought that her trip was somehow related to my client's case.

An hour before my mother's train departed I was already on the highway to Namcheon. And when she appeared at the taxi stop after having gotten off the train there, I was waiting for her a short distance away in my rented car. She immediately got in a taxi and I immediately followed behind. The cab drove slowly through the town and soon away from it. The streets weren't busy so it was easy to follow her. After about twenty minutes driving, we were traveling on a road in the countryside. It was a narrow, curvy road and some sections were unpaved. Forests and orchards lined both sides. I opened the window a bit and fresh air rushed into the car. I breathed in deeply and inhaled the scent of grass. There wasn't much traffic so I followed her taxi at a good distance but I didn't worry about losing sight of the cab. *Where is she going?* I wondered. The taxi continued on its way, but no towns or villages appeared.

Finally, the taxi stopped on a hilltop overlooking the ocean. The sunlight reflecting off the water dazzled my eyes. It looked like millions of shining fish scales. "Ah!" I exclaimed, shocked to emerge from the forest to see the ocean. It was as if the wild forest had opened its heart and had revealed a vast ocean inside. The perception that the ocean was tucked inside the forest reminded me of the myths that claim every forest is sacred and every forest has the beginning of the world inside it. In legends, the forest is always a sanctuary where its sacred trees should be worshiped.

The taxi stopped and Mother got out so I had to drive past them on the road. My mother turned as I drove by and looked at my car as I sped away. Even though I had concealed my face behind sunglasses, I was afraid she had recognized me and I was scared she would run after me shouting out my name. I panicked and without looking into the rearview mirror, I pressed down on the accelerator. Like an unthinking colony of lemmings leaping from a cliff, I abruptly turned off the road and drove toward the ocean. Of course I wasn't a lemming, so I stopped just before plunging into the water. I let out a deep sigh.

At a nearby beachfront shop I bought a bottle of soda and drank it before heading back up the hill to the road. But the taxi and my mother were nowhere in sight. I realized that the spot where they had stopped was a trailhead. The path leading into the mountains was too narrow and steep to drive on. Tall grass lined both sides of it and beyond the grass was dense forest. Since I couldn't see anything else around, I had to assume that my mother had followed the trail into the mountains. But I had no idea why Mother would have taken the trail or where it would lead me.

I left the car on the hilltop and brushing aside the tall grass, I made my way along the trail. I wondered if my mother was just ahead of me on the trail and where she could be going. I moved forward cautiously. The steep trail made an abrupt turn and the land became level. I turned around and saw the sea in the distance once again dazzling my eyes with its shining scales. I felt giddy at the change of scenery offered again by the break in the forest. The ocean seemed to rise up to the sky and seagulls flew in every direction. The horizon seemed far, far away.

Further on, the trail led to a steep cliff that dropped down to the water, and to my disbelief, there was a house at the edge of the cliff. A handsome palm tree, which seemed to rise hundreds of meters up into the sky, stood in front of the house. Perched on the cliff, the tree looked much taller than it actually was. If its roots were as long as its trunk, I imagined that they must have penetrated down through the cliff and dipped their feet in the ocean water.

Its huge fronds stuck out in all directions like a giant windmill wheeling among the clouds. It was a marvelous sight, something out of a painting, or a dream. I knew, though, it was neither a painting nor a dream. I stepped forward. But the scene still looked unreal. Hiding myself behind a wide oak tree, I looked down at the palm tree and the house on the cliff. From this angle they appeared to be floating on the ocean. The palm tree resembled a mast and the house looked like a ship about to sail on a sea voyage. I wondered if my mother was aboard. I repressed the urge to run down to the house and satisfy my curiosity.

The palm tree stood out among all the other trees to such an extent that I began to wonder how a palm could have even gotten there. As someone who had never traveled overseas, this was the first real palm tree I had ever seen. I was jumping to conclusions by even calling it a palm, I had only seen them on TV or in books. I didn't think that palm trees were even able to grow in Korea but somehow this tree felt like it belonged here. The surreal scene of the house and the huge foreign tree on the edge of the cliff began to feel like some kind of hallucination. I suddenly felt very thirsty and I imagined myself climbing barechested up the tree trunk to the top and breaking open a coconut to gulp down the juice inside.

I had been staring at the scene for a while when I detected movement under the tree. My mouth was still dry with anxiety but instead of the coconut juice I had to swallow my saliva. Two people had appeared. One of them seemed to be helping the other person, a man, who walked very slowly as if he were injured or ill. The sick man looked like a scarecrow. The baggy clothes he wore couldn't fully conceal an emaciated body of skin and bones. The two people walked toward the palm tree, following its long shadow. Everything seemed to move in slow motion, as if the heat of the sun had dissolved time. They stopped when they reached the base of the tree.

The person who helped the frail man was a woman. And without using my binoculars, I recognized that it was my mother. She helped the man lie down with his head raised slightly on a wooden platform under the tree. The palm tree's long shadow covered the man's body like a blanket. Wind from the ocean stirred up their hair.

It was an idyllic scen. They looked as if they were lounging on the deck of a yacht that was about to set sail. The churning ocean created endless waves below.

After watching the scene for a bit longer I was able to make out more details. The man had an unruly beard and his pale face was wrinkled but looked peaceful, and I could just detect a faint smile. Sitting next to him on the platform, Mother looked up at the palm tree. Soon the two of them were staring up at the tree. She gestured toward it as she spoke to him. The waves continued to break like fangs piercing the face of the cliff.

My mother touched the man's face affectionately. Watching her tender movements, it occurred to me that the hands are the most effective means of conveying emotion. The way she moved showed such familiarity and tenderness that even as a distant viewer, I felt a tingling sensation spread throughout my body. Her hands, charged with love, caressed the man's hair, ears, eyes, and lips. And as her hands passed over him, his face glowed like a golden sun.

Soon she stood up and walked behind the palm tree. The tree concealed her completely, almost as if she had slipped inside its slender trunk. But she soon appeared from behind the tree. And she was naked! Naked, as if just born. Surrounded by nature and without any clothes on, she looked like Eve in the Garden of Eden. And she didn't seem to have any sense of shame, again like Eve in Eden. She moved in a light and agile manner as if she were dancing without touching the earth. The man gazed at her with an expression of deep contentment and affection. Gracefully, she lay down next to him and they embraced. Then she raised her body and lowered herself on to his. Her face, bosom, arms, palms, and lips all rested on his. Each body was symmetrical to the other and together they seemed to form one whole, as perfectly symmetrical as a tree. They looked natural and beautiful and even sacred as if they had finally become complete again after a long separation. I wasn't sure why, but I didn't feel disgusted at the sight of them, or reproachful of their actions, or ashamed for watching them. Perhaps it was the influence of the exotic tree, which seemed to pass from sky to earth and into the ocean and even further down into a world below.

I was as detached as if I had been watching a scene in a movie. The real world in which I stood was ugly but they seemed to be outside reality in a world that was pure and chaste. I set down my binoculars.

I spread out on the ground between the trees. Thorns pricked into my back but I didn't move. Locusts and grasshoppers and other bugs crawled all over my body but I let them be. *Yes, let them be* I said to myself before I finally stood up. As I turned to walk back down the mountain, I glanced one last time toward the palm tree. I saw them lying motionless but still bound together. I felt as if I had been hypnotized or was having a daydream.

Unable to decide whether to return to Seoul or not, I drove to the end of the road and there, at a dusty beachfront store, I was drinking a lukewarm soda when Mother called me on my cell phone. "Ki-hyeon, are you there?" Mother asked.

Hearing her deep, calm voice, my heart sank like a book dropped from a shelf. It struck the ground with a thud. "Yes . . . it's me . . ." I stuttered. I couldn't conceal my embarrassment. She must have known that I had followed her to Namcheon. She asked me where I was and I froze up immediately. Her voice was so calm and normal that I again wondered if the scene I'd witnessed in the mountains had been a hallucination.

I didn't know how to answer but she continued, "Do you think you could drive your brother to Namcheon today?"

"Bring him today?"

"Yes," she answered curtly.

"But why?" I asked.

Her response was terse, "You'll find out why when you get here."

I realized then that I was needlessly worried. Mother seemed not to know that I was in Namcheon. Of course, she could've been bluffing, but her voice was sincere and solemn and even a bit sad. Letting out a sigh of relief, I quickly calculated the time needed to travel from Namcheon to Seoul and back. It would be a good four hours to Seoul if I got on the highway immediately. And with another four hours needed to return with my brother, it would mean a total of eight hours driving. It would be almost impossible for me to get to Seoul and back to Namcheon before the day ended.

Now back to my usual self, I told her that I wouldn't be able to make it that day since I was not in Seoul. Mother told me to set out early the following morning. When I asked her where in Namcheon she was, she gave me a phone number, saying, "Call me when you arrive." I jotted down the number.

"Is everything okay with you?" I asked, as if I still knew nothing.

"You'll find out when you get here," she answered and then hung up without further explanation.

18

My brother refused to travel to Namcheon, demanding to know why he should have to go somewhere he had never been before without being given any reason. When I explained what Mother had told me, he became even more hostile and stubborn. Considering how closed off he was, it wasn't easy for him to travel to a strange place without even knowing why. My brother hadn't been born so reserved and antisocial. As in many cases, before the accident he was much more active and adventurous. I tried to persuade him to change his mind, describing Mother's somber tone when she had requested the trip, but he was unshakable. I had the impression that he was suspicious of me and felt the need to be cautious of my attempt to persuade him. He pressed me for information about Mother's purpose and when I couldn't answer, he sneered angrily at me, his lips twitching. "Why don't you go alone," he said. His expression and tone of voice suggested that he was really saying "You can't fool me." Again I told him that it was only him that Mother wanted to see in Namcheon, not me, and that I was just meant to be his driver. But my brother refused to change his mind.

I went to my father's room to seek his help. After listening to me, Father showed great interest, even raising his head from his ba-duk game and looking directly up at my face. "Are you saying your mother's in Namcheon now?" he asked. I winced, but pretending not to know anything, I answered that she had said she was in Namcheon and I asked him who she might know that lived there. Father thought for a moment and then, as if he had suddenly made an important decision, he got up and went into my brother's room. I followed him. Father gently called out my brother's name and then said, "You should go. Someone is waiting for you."

This was all he said, but I knew that he had succeeded in convincing him to go. My brother tried to respond but Father had already left the room.

The very questions that my brother had asked were also on my mind. What I had seen that day came back to me, like a scene in a dream: the picturesque house on the cliff overlooking the ocean, the palm tree, and the two people under it. Father's reaction made me think that he knew everything: the reason Mother wanted my brother in Namcheon, why she had gone there, who the man with her was, and the kind of relationship the two of them had. I knew I wouldn't be able to sleep that night with all these unanswered questions nagging at me.

I assumed Father would be in his room, but instead, he was in the garden. It wasn't strange to see him tending the plants, but it was odd to see him in the garden at night. Holding the door open, I watched him for a while as he watered the plants. The darkness pressed in around him, his curved back made him look old and sad. My heart was flooded with sympathy for him. Had he ever been happy? For some reason he had never looked happy and he certainly didn't look happy now.

People say a third person never really knows what's going on between a husband and wife, but everyone who knew my parents noticed that my mother wasn't very warm or affectionate toward my father and come to think of it, my father acted the same way toward my mother. I never saw them talk about the news, for example, or playfully exchange jokes. It wasn't a tense relationship either, but this could mean that a serious problem existed. The indifference, the minimal dialogue, and noninterference in each other's lives must be the worst scenario in a relationship. In that case, my mother must've also been unhappy in her married life. But after having witnessed the scene between my mother and the strange man, I had deeper sympathy for my father. I felt a strong impulse to tell him what I had seen in Namcheon. But I soon thought that acting on my emotions would've been inconsiderate and rash, and I had decided not to be that kind of person, so I tried to rein in my impulse. Mother had taken off all her clothes. Under the palm tree that shot up into the sky from the cliff, its roots sunk in the ocean floor, my naked mother, feeling no shame, like Eve in the Garden of Eden, had sat naked atop a strange man. But somehow it seemed that there was nothing shameful in their act. The bizarre scene, two incomplete bodies finally becoming whole, had reminded me of a sacred ritual. Maybe it had not been a hallucination or a dream, but a strange ritual. But what was the ritual for?

"Father, who is it that's waiting?" I asked, moving closer to him. He continued what he had been doing in the garden, as though he hadn't noticed that I was right beside him. "You said . . . he should go and that someone was waiting in Namcheon. But when you said it, it didn't sound like it was Mother who was waiting for him . . . it didn't seem like you were referring to Mother when you said that. I had the impression that you knew something we didn't. You seemed to know why Mother went to Namcheon and why she wanted us to go there. Are you . . ." Father had turned and placed his pointer finger on his lips, signaling for me to stop speaking. He then reached out to caress a leaf on a nearby tree. I wondered why he had silenced me but I thought it best not to ask more questions.

Father mumbled something as he gently held the leaf. He was talking to the tree. But I couldn't make out what he was saying, and, of course, the tree couldn't hear him either. At that moment, as if correcting what I was thinking, Father said in a calm voice, "Trees also have emotions. Touch this leaf."

"That's crazy," I muttered to myself, but his tone was serious. Perhaps I'd never known that Father had a strong relationship with nature even though he'd always devotedly tended his garden. I put my hand on the leaf. "All I feel is the cool night air."

"You have to show love and trust to the tree," he advised me.

"How?" I asked, still skeptical.

"It should come from your heart," he explained. "While holding the leaf, whisper that you love it. Plants can sense your emotions through your hands."

He seemed so serious and I wanted to believe him. So I whispered to the tree that I loved it. But I still didn't feel anything. The tree didn't seem to hear my confession of love and it didn't look like it would ever react to my words. Even if the tree had in fact possessed emotions and it had been able to react to me, it wouldn't have made much difference. I didn't have what it took to understand its feelings. It takes two to communicate.

Father said that eventually the leaf's rough skin would become as soft and warm as human skin. I waited but nothing happened. I told him that I didn't feel any change.

"Plants can read human minds," he explained, as serious as if he were giving a science lesson. "It's inexplicable, but I've heard that plants have keen awareness, beyond the five senses. I once read an article about oak trees trembling in fear as a woodman approached and about red radishes becoming pale with terror as a rabbit neared. Yes, plants are alive with emotions. They feel pain, sadness, and happiness. And they know by instinct whether a person lies or speaks the truth. A feigned love doesn't provoke a reaction from them. As with people, you should be truthful when communicating with plants."

I tried hard to be truthful and to truly love the tree. But the leaf didn't become soft and warm. Nothing happened. Father moved on to another tree. He again mumbled something to it, but I couldn't make it out. I also moved to a new tree and again tried to convey my love to it. But loving a tree wasn't easy for me so I feared that receiving any friendly reaction, or any reaction at all from it, would be impossible. To tell the truth, I didn't believe what Father had said. It was a different matter, though, from whether I generally understood him or not. Trying to communicate with plants was absurd and irrational, like trying to communicate with aliens. I quickly withdrew my hand from the tree. Father froze, perhaps detecting my doubts. Standing motionless, he almost looked like one of the trees he had been talking to.

In an attempt to put an end to this absurd and irrational game, I changed my tone of voice, "But Father, you haven't told me why we have to go to Namcheon." This sentence sounded a little too blunt as I tried to break the mystical atmosphere he was creating in the garden. But Father, in keeping with his usual manner, didn't seem to feel any need to answer my question. I suddenly felt that there was a great distance between the two of us, as if my father were a stranger from a foreign land. The garden itself felt like a different world, a place where I didn't belong. I felt uncomfortable there and I didn't want to stay any longer. I stepped away from Father and the trees and went inside.

That night I dreamed that my father had turned into a palm tree. Branches came out of his body and leaves covered his head. Penetrating the thick layers of the earth, his roots reached deep underground, passing through a soft sedimentary layer and then a hard rocky layer until finally reaching the ocean where they sank into the water while his trunk rose upward into the sky. I saw the windmill-like fronds at the top of his trunk. The palm tree stood atop a steep cliff overlooking the ocean. And the tree's shadow raced to the end of the world. A naked man and woman lay down under him. They were thrusting their bodies into each other's. The man entered the woman and the woman entered the man. And they finally became one. A palm frond fell down and covered their body. I woke up and pushed my blanket away.

19

The surreal image of the palm tree on the seaside cliff stayed in my mind and motivated me to bring the camera on our trip. I thought that my brother would be unable to resist the urge to take photos once he saw the scenery. We weren't exactly in a holiday picnic mood but on the road to Namcheon I was excited about the possibility that the location would inspire my brother to take pictures. But I still didn't know what awaited us and I couldn't help feeling uneasy and anxious about it.

My brother didn't say a word throughout the entire four-hour trip. His withdrawal after his latest fit was much deeper than usual. He refused to look directly at me. As soon as I had helped him into the car, he closed his eyes and seemed to fall asleep. But sleeping soundly in a speeding car wasn't easy for him. He tossed about frequently. He must've noticed the camera on the seat beside me but he didn't show any sign that he had seen it. I became impatient and wanted to talk to him. I had two secrets that he was unaware of and both of them related to him. Just two days before, I had spoken with his ex-girlfriend and the following day I had gone to Namcheon and seen our mother with a strange man. But I didn't feel it was the right time to talk about any of this with my brother.

Upon arriving in Namcheon, I called the number Mother had given me. A man answered, but he immediately asked me to hold for a second and handed the phone over to my mother. "Where are you?" she asked. I gave her the name of a prominent landmark in town. She began to give me directions to where she was but since I already knew how to get there I didn't pay much attention. She asked me to stop the car on a hill where I could see the ocean and said "I'll be waiting for you there."

I did as instructed. "Here we are . . . isn't it beautiful?" I asked my brother, as I stopped the car. He opened his eyes slightly and looked down at the ocean.

"Yes, we're here," he said. It was strange, but the way he said it gave me the impression that he had been here before. But I immediately dismissed the idea; my brother couldn't also have a client who'd asked him to follow his mother.

I got out of the car and saw Mother standing nearby, staring blankly at the car. Maybe it was my imagination but she looked thinner and paler than she had the day before. She appeared to be preoccupied with something, only halfway paying attention to her surroundings. It was hard to face her with the memory of her naked body still fresh in my mind.

Taking my brother's wheelchair out of the trunk, I called out loudly, "Mother, we're here." She finally acknowledged our presence and began walking toward us. I sat my brother in his wheelchair and Mother walked to the back of it and grasped the handles. As I closed the trunk, rolled up the window, and took the camera bag out of the car, she started off with the wheelchair up the path to the mountain. Soon the cliff and the house and the palm tree would appear. I thought it was about time she told us what was going on but her odd demeanor kept me from speaking out. My brother seemed to feel the same way as he started to say something but then hesitated and looked at me.

Entering a more difficult section of the trail with a steeper slope, the wheelchair gradually slowed down. I grasped the handles and told Mother that I would push. She turned to look at me as if she had totally forgotten that I was there. "Ki-hyeon, I think you . . ." she said, without finishing, and then turned her head away from me. There were beads of sweat on her forehead.

"Mother, what do you want to say? That I shouldn't come with you?" I asked. My question sounded rude even to me. Mother also seemed to take it that way as she sputtered out, "Well . . . it's not like that . . ." It was obvious that I was only there as my brother's driver, but I couldn't understand why. Mother was definitely not her usual self.

Before she could say anything, I took hold of the wheelchair's handles again. "Let's go, Mother," I said, as I forcefully pushed the wheelchair forward. "While we're walking, please tell us where we are and why we're here."

She paused for a second but after a few steps she asked if Father had said anything to me. I remembered his words from the previous night about plants and their emotional life, but it was clear that she wasn't asking about that. I shook my head.

"I wish he had told you something . . ." Mother said. I detected a tinge of disappointment toward my father in her voice. I almost said he had tried to tell me something but I kept quiet since I wasn't really sure what Father had meant to say.

"I want you to meet someone," Mother finally said. She then became silent.

This time my brother pressed her for an answer, "Who?" he asked.

"It's someone . . . neither of you know," she answered, her voice trembling.

"But who?" I asked.

"He's left this world," she said, her voice still quaking.

"Who's the person?" my brother asked again, his words charged with unusual force. At that moment the answer to the question was the only thing my brother and I wanted to know. From his tone of voice, it seemed like my brother had some idea about whom we would be meeting. And perhaps he could sense that I did as well.

The ocean came into view, glittering wildly in the sun as it reflected the vast sky. The palm tree stood tall and straight as it punctured the heavens.

"Ah," my brother gasped, shielding his eyes from the blinding sun. "Where are we?" he asked as he raised his palms to his cheeks in amazement. Immediately, I understood that bringing the camera had been a good idea. I was excited by the prospect of him taking photos again but I knew that I shouldn't do or say anything hasty because this was not the time to stir up his emotions again. I stopped walking and so did my mother. We all now shifted our gazes from the ocean to the palm tree and up toward its canopy.

"He planted that palm tree . . ." Mother said. Her voice was calm and even but her eyes were wet with tears.

20

"He planted that palm tree." No words immediately followed, as if they were trapped in her throat. Mother looked as if she were faced with some chore that she wanted to avoid. She also looked as if she were being coerced into making a confession. For a moment I thought that she might be expecting a show of sympathy but quickly dismissed the idea. Mother knew that penance cannot be avoided, regardless of how much we want to; it's determined by life and determined by destiny. Since she had already made a decision about what had to be done, sympathy was not what she needed. All we could do was wait for her words, lodged in her throat like bones. We could do nothing to lessen the penance that was hers alone.

We waited for her to reveal the secret she had hidden from us for such a long time. We were curious to hear the words that stuck in her throat like bones but they couldn't be dislodged by force. I understood this, as did my brother. As if it were the only means to get Mother to make her confession, my brother and I bore the long and heavy silence until Mother was finally ready. Finally she sat down on the ground, relaxing her tightly wound nerves. The grass, as stiff as well ironed linen, crumpled beneath her. She put her hand to her forehead, as if she felt dizzy, and let out a faint groaning sound. An uneasy feeling made me tighten my grip on the wheelchair's handles. The palm, a tree from distant lands, reached into the sky creating an otherworldly atmosphere on the cliff above the seashore.

"How to begin . . ." she said, looking like she was at her wit's end and didn't know what to do. To me, though, her struggle was a sign that she was now finally about to make her confession. I was right. With the attitude of someone performing a difficult task, she began to pull the bones from her throat.

"I met him working at the Dandelion." She was trying to make it clear that she intended to clear up all the secrets of her private life. The maxim "The part is the whole" fits in this case. Uncovering the secret, even though it was only a part, is the same as uncovering the whole. The hidden part is always larger than the exposed. Mother owns the Dandelion now, but that she had once worked there when she was young was something we all knew. The fact that at the restaurant she had first met the man who had planted the palm tree was not known to us.

"I was twenty-one then," she said, looking up at the sky. My brother stared down at the ground and I looked toward the ocean. We avoided each other's eyes like criminals waiting to be sentenced. When she said, "I was twenty-one then" I felt like something dropped from my heart with a thud. What was it? Why did my heart fall when she spoke as if she was being forced to make a confession? I felt that her confession wouldn't be solely about her. I was seized by the thought that her confession would sentence us too.

"Back then I wasn't familiar with city life and didn't know much about the world," she said. "My world was too narrow." Tears sprang to her eyes as she began to talk about her father who never earned his own living but arrogantly bragged about the old days when he ruled over many servants, a father who was a drinker, a gambler, and a liar, and who in addition was restless in his later years, wandering about everywhere, so much so that he didn't even know his wife had died until he eventually returned to live off of his twenty-one-year-old daughter. She recounted that period of her life in order to explain how she had ended up working at the Dandelion. One day, when she was in college, making her living as a tutor for the insolent and lazy son of a nouveau-rich family, her father reappeared, and he was ill. Obliged to help him, she had quit her studies. It would have been more difficult for her to ignore her father than to discontinue her education. If only her father hadn't been sick, she said, or if only he could've at least moved about freely, she might've turned him away. But I knew she couldn't have done that under any circumstances. She couldn't ignore her own father because her world was too circumscribed. She said so herself.

And the limits of someone's world cannot move beyond their understanding of that world.

Upon being informed by a distant relative of her father's return, my mother hurriedly went back to her hometown and saw him, his body and spirit now in such shambles that she wondered how he had even made it back home. There wasn't one single part of him, physically or mentally, that was normal or healthy. She quickly got him to a hospital in a nearby city and quit school. She had no other choice. But still, she didn't have enough money. The only people she knew with money were the parents of her lazy student. Since she couldn't see any other way, she asked them for help. Although the boy's parents were fond of her since her tutoring had enabled their son to do a little better at school, borrowing money from them was still a lot to ask and it took great courage on my mother's part.

"I'm sorry but we just can't," said the student's father. Contrary to his sympathetic words, his face showed that he really didn't care. She felt helpless.

But the man's wife scrutinized Mother's face and body and then suddenly said, as if tossing bait in front of her, "There is one way." She then asked Mother, "How about working for us at our business?" Mother didn't know what kind of business they ran; she had never been interested in how they made their money. She asked the woman what kind of work was involved, though this didn't necessarily mean that her decision would be affected by the answer. At the time getting money had been her primary concern and everything else was secondary. She thought that securing a job in addition to borrowing money to help her father would be another feather in her cap. "We run a high-class downtown establishment. Dandelion is the name of it. It's an exclusive restaurant and not just anyone can patronize it. It's a place for people, mainly gentlemen, with money and power. If you can work a cash register we can offer you a job. It's not easy to find trustworthy help." The woman then paid Mother a few compliments and offered her an advance on the condition that she pay back what she owed over time by working at the Dandelion. The woman then extended a generous offer, "I'll give you enough money now to help with your father's medical expenses and for you to rent a two bedroom house." Mother was touched by her offer and thanked her profusely.

A week later she began working at the Dandelion. She worked the cash register for two months but the job was too easy, just running the register and keeping records, with lots of free time, but her salary was small. Consequently, she couldn't even pay down the interest on the money she had borrowed, never mind her father's ongoing medical expenses. As her debt grew larger day by day, she didn't see how she would ever be able to pay it down.

In the same manner as when she said "There is one way" the woman threw a new and enticing offer at Mother's feet, telling her that she could make more money if she worked the tables. It was true. Not only were the wages higher but the wealthy customers were very generous with pretty waitresses and the tips amounted to more than the salary. Rumor had it that one woman at the restaurant had received a new house as a tip for her services. All the other workers envied the woman who herself didn't deny it and so my mother believed the rumor. She considered her debt along with her father's mounting hospital bills, which she wasn't able to pay. The financial strain burdened her greatly and she couldn't free herself of it. After three months working at the cash register, she started waitressing. She was still twenty-one.

21

That year she met a man at the Dandelion. It took a while for her to get to know him since she really didn't have any interest in the restaurant's customers. She didn't make an effort to get to know anyone in particular but over time she got to know some of them. People who came into the restaurant with the man addressed him as "Mr. Secretary." She didn't have any idea what such a title might have meant. To her he was just one of the Dandelion's many customers.

But for some time, this man had showed a particular interest in Mother. Whenever he went to the Dandelion, he called for her. Of course, he had been a regular customer even before she began working there, so it wasn't as if he came to the restaurant only to see her, at first anyway. He would come in with a couple of other men, sometimes more, for dinner and they would spend two or three hours dining and drinking. At times he would stay until after midnight, but this was rare. Even when he started coming more frequently, it wasn't so much as to seem unusual. He had always been a regular customer who might visit the Dandelion frequently for a time and then not show up again for six months. But when he began to show up every night and sit drinking until late, the change caught everyone's attention. The fact that his new habits had come about because of my mother was first noticed by the restaurant employees and soon also by the customers. Mother became the target of jealousy and gossip.

He was a taciturn man who liked to drink but rarely got drunk. When Mother filled his glass, he drank slowly and always offered her a drink. But he didn't force her to partake. No, he was never discourteous. And this made a positive impression on Mother, who by then had become weary of customers forcing her to drink and flirting with her under the pretext of being drunk. But the two of them didn't talk to each other that much. Usually, he would just gaze at her affectionately as he had dinner or drinks in silence, and then he would leave. Some days he only stayed twenty minutes or so if that was all the time he could afford. Everyone at the Dandelion knew that he came in every day just to see her, regardless of how busy he was.

As opposed to other customers, he wasn't demanding and he never did anything to make my mother feel uncomfortable. If he had ever even hinted at his love for her while drunk, she would've ignored him. He never employed any of the tactics that men use when they want to win over a woman. The most he ever wanted from her was to rest his head on her lap after having a few drinks in a private room. And when they got to know each other better, she consented. Lying against her lap with his eyes closed, he looked like a child. His face became peaceful; all the tension he carried while his eyes were open had vanished. At those times she felt empathy for the man, a man who was too busy to even get a good night's sleep. She was happy that she could provide him with such a respite, even if only a short one. When he awoke looking refreshed after a short nap, she was pleased. She learned to feel happiness through offering her lap as his resting place. Love came to her slowly, like a flower that blooms unaware. Was it love? If not, what was it?

One night he came into the Dandelion. But Mother remembered that this night he was already drunk when he arrived. He was still able to stand and walk but he slurred his words when speaking. And as soon as he came in, he began to ask for one drink after another. Mother tried to persuade him to stop, telling him that he was drunk enough, but he was stubborn and kept drinking. For some unknown reason he was agitated that night. He said to himself "It's all over," and then shouted "You've got me wrong, I'm not a clown." He then told her "I'm ashamed of myself when I'm in front of you . . . I won't live as a coward any longer." His words were too incoherent for her to comprehend what he was trying to say. She also remembered that he tightly held her hand while speaking, so tightly that it felt like her circulation was being cut off.

Finally, he passed out on her lap. Never before had he been so sloppy because of overdrinking, but that night it soon became evident that his nap would not end within thirty minutes. Waking him up was inconceivable to her, but she couldn't let him sleep on her lap all night, so she made a bed for him in the private dining room. She then took off his jacket and socks and cleaned his feet. Taking care of him in this way, she realized how much she loved him. As if to justify her reasons for loving him, she said that she didn't know what he was like with other people but with her he was so sweet and childlike that she felt she had to protect him. It was this tenderness, not his social position or political power, which roused her love.

After awakening the following morning, the man sat speechless for a while, looking like he had lost half his soul. Having suddenly realized where he had slept, he was a little embarrassed. When Mother brought his breakfast in he didn't touch it. Since he looked like he was preoccupied with something, she didn't say a word. Thinking that he might need some time alone, she began to step back, but he called out for her. Remembering his voice clearly, she repeated her name the way he had said it that day. When he called her, his tone was soft and tender, as if his voice caressed her name. For some reason the sound of her name in his mouth electrified her. But she also felt a flash of sadness, like an ominous premonition.

She froze on the spot. With only her head turned toward him, she waited to hear what he had to say. But he didn't continue. After what was for her a long, suffocating silence, he finally asked her if she would spend some time with him. Now it was Mother who remained silent, surprised by his request. His eyes, which she recalled as resembling those of a sad and helpless animal dangling from the edge of a cliff, seemed eager for her to say yes. And she felt that he would indeed go over the edge if she didn't say yes to him. Propelled by this feeling, without thinking about the consequences, she nodded her head over and over in assent. He then thanked her and immediately stood up. "Let's go," he said, grasping her by the wrist. Overwhelmed by her feelings for him, she felt unable to free herself and she followed him out of the restaurant without even asking where they were going.

22

Sitting in the back seat of the car with my mother, he gave his driver directions. But she didn't care where they were going. She could have never imagined that they'd travel far outside of Seoul all the way to the south coast of Korea. She still had no idea what he wanted and what he was planning to do. She happily sat next to him and waited. In her mind there wasn't any room to ask him ordinary questions, like whether it was okay for him to take a day off from work. She felt that fate had unstoppable plans in store for her. It was true.

It was winter but Namcheon was warm. "We don't have snow here," he told her, "since the temperature never drops below freezing." The sun was glowing that day. Walking along the beach, they didn't feel the winter's coldness at all. "This is paradise, a place not of this world," he said. She nodded in agreement. And as if to prove his words, clusters of purple wildflowers appeared. "It's wonderful to see plants blooming during winter. No one knows about this place except for me," he said, and then added, "that's another way of saying that this isn't an ordinary place. It doesn't even exist for other people and that's why this is heaven."

Mother vividly recalled his every word and through them she understood him; she could read his heart in what he said. Namcheon was close to his home village. He said that when he was young and he was sent into the mountains to gather firewood, he would come to this spot and sit for long periods.

"Strange, but it was always warm and cozy here, even on cool and windy days. I liked to look down at the ocean from the cliff and, most of all, I liked the peace and solitude I felt. And I often said to myself that I would someday build a house here and come here to live. And a couple of years ago I remembered this place and came again." He said that he'd returned to find the place exactly as he had remembered it so he built a house there and it became his perfect hideaway. Whenever he felt he wanted to disappear, he would come to this spot alone and stay for days before returning to Seoul. Mother said that he kept repeating that the world couldn't follow him because the place didn't exist for others.

Suddenly, he asked Mother, "How about living here with me?" She remembered that when he said this his face looked sad and lonely. She couldn't respond immediately, not because she doubted the sincerity of his offer but because she was too surprised to answer. At that moment, as they were the only two people in that wild and unreal place, she felt a strong connection to him and she trusted him completely. The fact that he was already a married man and had a family was only true in the world outside. And they were beyond the limits of that world — they were in a place that didn't exist for other people. Thus, all the circumstances of that world were inconsequential. Maybe she would've answered if he had asked her one more time. But he didn't. He must've sensed that asking such a question was an insult to their love, to that place. Yes, such a ridiculous question could be asked only once. Instead, he offered his arms to her and her body responded. No word is more honest than a body. No word is more trustworthy than a body. When he hugged her, she felt that she was at home. She felt that his body was part of hers, that their two bodies were one.

"Aristophanes said that love is a desire to search for oneness through the joining of two bodies," he said, fusing his body to hers.

"And Plato wrote in the Symposium . . ." she added.

"Yes," he said, finishing her sentence, "in some ancient myth humans at first had two faces, four arms, four legs, and four eyes, and two reproductive organs. But when humans challenged the gods, Zeus, after pondering over the matter, divided humans into two halves."

"So people seek love in order to find their other halves. To find the lost half of their body and soul and to regain the original oneness, people love," she replied.

"Yes, that's the ultimate goal of love. But meeting your true other half isn't easy. And that's why this world is filled with unhappy people," he whispered to her, idly playing with her long hair.

"I'm happier now than anyone," she whispered back to him. He smiled. And as if it were the only way to prove his happiness, he made love to her. He wanted to achieve the oneness of the original body by combining his body with hers and she wanted to achieve the same by uniting her body with his. Their bodies felt the ecstasy of oneness, and they realized that in such a state the spirit and body also become one. They felt this realization physically, it flowed through their bodies and their understanding was deep and true.

Reaching this point of her story, Mother let out a deep sigh, as if she had difficulty breathing. I suddenly felt quite thirsty. I looked up at the sky and I imagined my brother must feel the same way under the bright sun. I closed my eyes against the glare and like tiny spherical microbes, white afterimages floated behind my eyelids. I wasn't sure if I believed everything my mother was saying but I couldn't interrupt her. Making a confession wasn't her obligation but her right. My brother and I had the duty to listen to her. I couldn't speak for my brother, but her story made me uncomfortable, and I wished I could stop her from continuing, but I understood that I didn't have the right to do so. I looked at my brother who had his mouth firmly sealed as he stared out at the bright ocean. Mother followed his gaze for a moment but then, blinded by the sunlight, looked away. Her eyes stopped at the top of the palm tree. It wasn't difficult to see that she had already slipped into a different time period—she was trapped in the past.

"I wanted to live here. I didn't want that happiness to ever end," she said in a wistful voice. That winter when she was twenty-one she didn't feel any need to analyze time. Time stopped for her. She recalled that she didn't have any sense of how much time had passed while she was with him and she repeated her claim that time did not exist in this place. She said that the latitude line, which represented time, had been deleted from this spot and it was impossible to place a coordinate with only the longitude line, which represented space. She seemed to firmly believe what the man had said, that this place was of another world.

But eventually time had to resume its flow and soon an incident occurred that dashed their hopes of remaining outside the real world. Transcending this world is only something that happens in dreams. One day a black sedan appeared. Men in black suits got out of the car and were at first very courteous. They seemed to speak to the man about some serious matter. It was obvious that they were trying to persuade him of something, but she had no idea what. His driver, who had brought the men in black, stood to one side. Appearing to regret his incredible betrayal, the driver couldn't face his boss. But he apologized to Mother, saying "I'm so sorry." She could tell from his sincerity that he'd had no choice but to cooperate and that he was not to be blamed. She was certain that he would've only revealed their whereabouts after a harsh interrogation. Her man stubbornly resisted the men and they soon became physical. They shoved him into the black sedan and Mother was also forced to get in.

The car raced to Seoul, the center of the world they had left behind. The man gripped her hand. Mother didn't know what was happening, but she was determined to remain devoted no matter what. At that moment her trust in him was so deep and sincere that she would've died for him if he had asked her to. As they sped toward reality he confessed that he had lived a dishonest life. "If I told you what I've done in my life," he said, "you'd be shocked. But I won't live like that any longer. You've opened my eyes and you're my last hope."

She had so many questions to ask him but instead, showing her trust in her man, she simply embraced him. She had no interest in politics at all. She was only interested in him. And through body language she communicated that there was no need to speak—their love was beyond words.

She tried to control her emotions as she was told to get out of the car once they had reached Seoul. "I'm your hope and you're mine. I'll always be there for you," she said to him. Tears welled up in her eyes and he gave her his handkerchief. She wiped away her tears and then folded the handkerchief and held it tightly in her hand. She didn't know then that it was the beginning of a long separation but she had a gut feeling that things would never be the same. She recalled that she became hysterical after the car had left her behind. It had started out as a silent cry, like a trickle of tears, but soon turned into a sob like a cascading waterfall, and finally, it became a wailing that knocked her to the ground. She was experiencing the realization of her premonition.

23

"After that I didn't see him for a long time," Mother said, her sadness at the memory was evident. I had the impression that another trickle of tears was forming inside her which could easily turn into a cascade and then a mournful wailing. I knew it wasn't the time to ask any questions, but I had to distract her from her boiling emotions. "How long was a long time?" I asked her.

"Until yesterday," she replied, before again retreating into silence.

At that moment I understood that her sadness, which rose from the depths of her memory, was blocking her words. Following suit, I remained silent. But a voice inside me gasped, *That long!* Mother stared off into the distance. It was obvious that she was trying to conquer her emotions as they threatened to overcome her. Fearing a total breakdown, we did not press her. Making a confession was her right, and she didn't need to be pressured by her sons.

A long time passed before she finally resumed speaking. "After he left me, he never came back." And he no longer showed up at the Dandelion either. She hadn't received any word from him, but there were rumors. First, rumor had it that he had lost his position in politics. People also said that he was not only removed from his position but that he had been thrown in jail after being investigated for some unknown charges. Some people said that he had been imprisoned and others that he had been hospitalized. Rumors also circulated that he had been tortured and that this led to either his physical or mental deterioration. Some said that he was a broken man while others said he was exiled overseas. And some even declared him dead. The rumors varied so wildly that none of them were reliable. The few Dandelion customers who knew the truth about his situation kept silent. They were intentionally evasive when they spoke to Mother, and they seemed eager to avoid her entirely.

Finally, when she was in the fifth month of pregnancy, she was able to gather some reliable news from the driver who had come to Namcheon with the men in black suits. After some hesitation, he said that he didn't know much, but, nevertheless, he shared the little information that he had with Mother. His affection and sympathy for his boss was evident and he was proud of his loyalty. Based on what the driver said, the man had been accused of a very serious offense. It had been only a few years prior that the anticommunist law had been established to secure peace and liberty by blocking communist activities that were supposedly a danger to the nation's security. It was ironic that he, once the chief officer of the department immediately under the president, was now being prosecuted by the same department. The driver assured Mother that everything he told her was true. "I don't know that much but . . ." the driver said repeatedly as he continued to explain how the man had been charged with leaking national secrets. This confidential information had been divulged by a pro-North Korean, extremist organization whose aim was to create chaos in South Korea under secret orders from the North. In addition it was claimed that the man had been a spy for this organization. The driver's words sent a chill through her. "I don't know the details but I'm sure that he's still under arrest," the driver concluded, before hastily departing.

Just a few days later newspaper articles began to appear stating that a group of former political figures, students, and laborers were arrested for plotting an insurrection. She didn't see his photo in the newspapers which displayed the faces of the insurgents like the family tree of a criminal organization. But this didn't give her any relief. She had no idea what was really happening to him and the situation was unbearable for her. It was terrifying to think that a man could disappear without any trace. In addition to her love for him, she had another reason to find him — she was carrying his child. She visited anyone she could think of who might've known his whereabouts. But it was useless. Information about him was impossible to come by.

A few months later she finally received news of him from the owner of the Dandelion who had heard it from a reliable source.

His words made her heart ache with love and longing.

"I heard that he had divorced his wife," the restaurant owner had told her, "and you know, he was successful politically only because of his wife's family. His now ex-father-in-law is a powerful political figure. It's hard to believe that he would walk away from that golden opportunity. How dumb. I know, and everyone knows, that his ex-wife is a shrew who treated him terribly. But even so, what's the big deal? He should've just let her bitch about whatever she wanted to. Who the hell cares? What's so difficult about living like that? Well, I know he was extra kind to you . . . yeah, I heard that he has a loyal lover's heart. But I don't see that as a desirable trait for a man with great political ambition. Anyway, I heard that he left his wife, saying that he wasn't going to continue living in such a shameful way any longer. Well, I think highly of his courage, but was his life really so horrific? And again, he didn't succeed just because of his own ability but because of his wife's family. So, if I were him, I would've just shut my mouth and eaten whatever insult I was fed if it meant I could stay in power. What his wife brought to the table wasn't just peanuts, you know. Anyway, I don't get it. And this is solely my assumption, but I think all the accusations against him are nonsense. It all happened because he left his wife. And this I call putting a noose around your own neck. To the person who holds the knife, it's as easy to kill a man as it is to spare him, and in his case, his wife had the knife. Since it had been so easy for her family to make him successful, it would also be just as easy for them to destroy him. He must've known the destructive capacity of their power, even I know it. And that's the reason I don't understand why he had to dig his own grave. I really don't get it. And I know he cherished you. But listen, if they discover that you're somehow involved in this, they won't just leave you alone. It's just my thinking, but I'm probably right. So this is my advice to you—for your own sake, stop searching for him and forget about him. He's finished now. A dead man, I would say."

She didn't want to believe what she had heard and when she thought that she may have played a certain role in putting a noose around his neck, an uncontrollable yearning for him surged inside her. If the owner of the Dandelion's meandering monologue had been intended to free my mother from loving the man, his aim had failed. Instead, the owner's belief that the man was doomed had set fire to her heart. Now more than ever she understood that she couldn't just give up on him. The end of his former life was maybe a new beginning for the two of them. She continued making her desperate inquiries whenever she could, but she had to keep working every day at the restaurant until she was ready to give birth since she didn't have any other source of income.

"Expecting him to come and wait for me here in Namcheon, I came back to this place many times," Mother recalled. "But it was all in vain." Her memories were slow to come and charged with emotion. But like a wanderer who must move on, her confession continued, "And I gave birth to my first child here in Namcheon."

Her declaration sounded to me like the first sentence of Genesis. It was a proclamation similar to, "In the beginning God created the world." I felt like a bolt of lightning shot through my body and I now had to hold back my own tears. She had said it with a tinge of pride and power in her voice. Was it the pride of motherhood? Both my brother and I were left speechless. Did I look at my brother's face? I think I did, but I don't remember what kind of expression he wore. But Mother, wearing a proud face, like a seaman who has survived a dangerous storm before safely arriving at port, looked at her two sons in turn and repeated the words, "My first child." She had more to say and we would have continued to listen, but we didn't need any further explanation.

24

I don't have a clear memory of leaving Namcheon and returning to Seoul. The two days we spent in Namcheon felt like two years, or even twenty. The funeral was held under the palm tree and my brother and I burned incense for the departed soul. The memorial was quiet and low-key. Only a few people were there, and they spoke very little, as if they had all promised to remain silent. And maybe it was my imagination, but I felt that people were glancing at us and whispering to each other. Mother had squatted down alone in one corner. She looked like an improperly transplanted tree and this saddened me. To the family of the deceased my mother's position was unclear. My reason for being there was much less clear. It wasn't that my thoughts were disorganized but I was confused as I didn't know how I should feel. I wasn't sure if any of us, including my mother, should have even been there to begin with.

Although the person among us who must've been the most confused was my brother, he appeared much calmer than me. Actually, I seemed to be the only one who was nervous, worried about him having a fit during the event. His outward composure was a total surprise. He burned incense, bowed deeply to the memory of the deceased, and stayed next to Mother, all without saying a word. He held her hand tightly, and he acted as if he had anticipated and prepared for all the things that had been revealed. For an instant an image of Mother's first child, who had given her such pride and strength in her life, flashed in my mind's eye, but it was hard to fully understand his reaction.

A couple of people recognized my mother and approached her to bow politely. This gave me a strange feeling. Among them, one old man in particular drew the attention of my brother and me. He was white-haired, wrinkled, and stooped. He recognized my mother immediately and without any hesitation, he approached her, knelt down in front of her, and began weeping. Holding his hands, Mother tried to get him to stand up, but he was unwilling to rise. Inevitably, Mother also knelt down.

The old man's crying was interspersed with phrases like, "It was my fault that those terrible things happened to the two of you." But it wasn't easy to make out his words through his sobs. It was clear that the old man was asking Mother for forgiveness and that he was releasing all the regrets he had kept within him for so many years. He repeated, over and over again, that he was the one to blame. He also said how he was ashamed of still being alive and not getting what he really deserved—death. But at the same time he didn't resist giving an excuse for his conduct. "But as you know," he said, "we all had a hard time back then."

I thought I knew who the old man was. He was the only other person who knew about Namcheon and the person who had led the men in black to their paradise, the place forgotten by the world where my mother and her man had savored supreme happiness. The men in black took them back into the real world. And Mother and her man learned that paradise cannot exist for long. Her lover had disappeared. Meanwhile, she gave birth to their child. More time passed but her man never returned. She couldn't understand the reasons for his absence, but she knew that she had to accept reality. And so she married another man and more time passed. Finally, after many years, she finally met her lover again in that same place, a place beyond this world.

"Not long ago, this gentleman here sent me a message asking me to come here to Namcheon," Mother told us. Upon being referred to, the old man wept harder, as if she were recounting a terrible sin that he had committed.

"I wanted to contact you much sooner but I wasn't allowed. He didn't want me to get in touch with you . . . and that's why . . ." the old man said, still weeping. He even bowed to my brother and me and this made us uncomfortable. "He said he wanted to stop his medical treatment. He then asked me to bring him home. He wanted to spend what time he had left in Namcheon . . . that was six months ago," the old man said, wiping away his tears.

"Thirty-five years has passed," Mother said, her voice filled with sorrow.

"During those years he always thought of you," the old man told her.

"I also never forgot him," Mother said.

"The world has changed, so he thought it would be okay to return home from overseas. But by then he was already very sick," the old man said. His voice sounded remorseful, as if he had somehow contributed to the illness of his former boss.

"He lived overseas as a political exile. And never mind coming back home, he wasn't even allowed to contact anyone," Mother said.

"I knew it would've been too dreadful if he had died without seeing you again, and I knew that I wouldn't be able to bear it for the rest of my life," the old man explained to Mother, "and so that's why I disregarded his wishes and contacted you. Oddly enough, he must've had some inkling that you would come. The morning you arrived, he had an unusually clear mind and even asked me to bathe him as soon as he woke up. Then he wanted me to sit him under the tree."

"How surprised I was when I saw the tree, so grand. I had come here several times ... but I had never noticed it here before ... strange," Mother said.

"He said the same, he was also surprised at seeing the tree. After he arrived here, he would often say, 'I can't believe this' when he looked up at the tree," the old man said.

"Yes, it's unbelievable. The tree's telling us that we can believe the unbelievable," Mother said.

"On nice days he would sit under the tree for a long time. And one day there he told me the story behind it," said the old man.

"We were walking along the seashore and we found a strange seed," Mother said, gazing at me and my brother in turn.

"And he thought it probably came from somewhere in Brazil or Indonesia," the old man added, enthusiastically.

"So we planted the palm seed in front of the house," Mother

continued. "We were experimenting to see if this tropical plant could grow here in our paradise." Letting out a sigh, she looked up at the tree.

She said that when they realized that the palm seed had crossed the Pacific Ocean to get there, they took it as some kind of symbol of their love. They felt somehow that their love depended on the fate of the tree. But she didn't really think the tree could survive in foreign soil. "The climate and conditions are so different . . ." Mother said. The sight of the palm tree, reaching proudly up toward the sky in an alien land, caused my mother's eyes to fill with tears.

The phrase "symbol of their love" stayed with me. I now understood the strange ritualistic atmosphere I had sensed when I saw my mother and her man beneath the tree. And I now vaguely understood why Mother's naked body had seemed so innocent and pure as she lay atop the emaciated old man, arms to arms, chest to chest, face to face, legs to legs.

Speeding back toward Seoul after the funeral, we all remained quiet in the car. Mother looked exhausted and my brother looked like he was deep in thought. The atmosphere was as heavy as lead. I drove, looking straight ahead. But the image of the tall palm tree that had traveled across the Pacific Ocean to stand on a cliff in Namcheon kept flashing into my mind, distracting me as I drove. The seed had hibernated in the earth for years until it was able to sprout in a foreign land, in an alien soil and climate. But it didn't just lie dormant in the earth all that time; it acclimatized itself until it was finally able to adjust to the conditions.

The tree's roots reach the ocean and the ocean caresses the tree. No, wait, it's the opposite, I thought. The tree caresses the ocean. And the tree is grand, its roots extending across the waters. I could picture the tree's long roots, deep under the ocean floor, reaching across the Pacific to the coastal jungle of Brazil or reaching Indonesia. I imagined the roots traveling back and forth under the ocean every night. That trees are immobile and rooted to one place is a terrible misconception. *Look at the palm tree that has crossed the Pacific! If a tree can journey to a land across an ocean, it should also be able to travel back. Trees are not immobile; it's just that their mobility is secret.* The presence of my mother and brother in the car didn't hinder my free and boundless imagination. But the heavy atmosphere lingered in the car. My brother looked exhausted and Mother appeared to be deep in thought. So I kept my wild ideas to myself and continued to stare at the road in front of me.

25

After returning home from Namcheon we resumed our normal habits. We were back to behaving as if we all lived alone. Every day Mother left early in the morning and came back late at night. My brother didn't come out of his room nor did my father. And we never ate together. One morning I heard our maid complaining, "What a crazy family!" as she prepared breakfast for the fourth time. She was right. And while our lack of communication may have become worse after our trip to Namcheon, our indifference toward one another had accumulated slowly, like dust piling up over time, layer upon layer, in the hard to reach places. What would have been strange and unnatural to others seemed perfectly normal to my family.

While we were in Namcheon my answering machine had faithfully collected a couple of messages. They were both calls for my Bees and Ants Agency. One of them was from a woman wanting to find her runaway daughter and the other was from a young man who wanted me to purchase roundtrip plane tickets for him to Jeju Island for the Christmas holidays. In fact, the man who wanted plane tickets left a second message, complaining in an angry voice about not receiving any response and asking if I was still in business or not, and then he uttered a few profanities before hanging up.

I had hoped for a message from Soon-mee, but she hadn't called. And there was no message from the client who had asked me to tail my mother. I was a bit disappointed. I thought maybe the bastard knew more about my family than I did, which bothered me and I had to find out what he knew and what he was trying to uncover. I should have pressed him about his motive. I couldn't believe it was a coincidence that he'd just happened to hire me, of all people. And if it wasn't just random chance, then what the hell was this all about? If he wanted me to gather information about my own mother while pretending he didn't know that I was her son, then it was clear there must've been some reason behind it. Maybe he knew Mother's secrets and he wanted me to know in order to expose her to her family. But what could he gain from that? If I could just find out who the bastard was I might be able to get some answers. I was now anxious to speak with him, but he hadn't contacted me, and I had no way to contact him.

Two days later Soon-mee left a message on my answering machine. My heart raced as I listened to it. I was still emotionally attached to her and this wasn't what I wanted at all. It pricked at my conscience. I knew her voice wouldn't leak out of my room and reach my brother, but regardless I was still apprehensive so I lowered the volume of the message. I knew that Soon-mee would never leave a message confessing her feelings for me, but being the miserable dog I was, I still remained hopeful. "It's Soon-mee," she said, pausing as if hesitant to say anything further. I held my breath. "I'd like to meet with you," she finally said and then again paused a moment before hurriedly backtracking. "Oh, never mind," she said before hanging up. I could understand her hesitation. She had mustered up all her courage but it wasn't enough to conquer all the doubts she must have. Yes, I could understand her. But why she had decided to reach out to me would remain a mystery until I met her.

Her doubts didn't dissuade me. Without giving it a second thought, I rushed out to find her. Before leaving home, I left my cell number on my answering machine message in case she called again while I was on my way. And I thought that there was little chance the woman who'd left the message about her runaway daughter would call again. But I had this obsessive feeling that I shouldn't miss a phone call from my existing client.

Soon-mee was sitting at the front desk when I entered the library. Maybe it was my imagination but she looked paler than she had before. Wearing gloomy look on her face, she never lifted her eyes from the keyboard. I cleared my throat in front of her. "May I have your library card?" she said, in a faint voice, still not looking up at me. I took my driver's license from my wallet and placed it down on her desk. After seeing my name and photo, she froze for a moment.

She stopped typing and her eyelashes trembled slightly.

Sliding my driver's license toward me, Soon-mee quietly stood up and walked away. I followed her. Her composed demeanor made me think that this time she had been expecting me. She went into the office but came out right away with her jacket on. The beige trench coat complemented her pale complexion. Outside, the street was bathed in sunlight. She winced, but I'm not sure if it was only from the sunlight.

We went into a small coffee shop near the library. Its low ceiling was made from raw timbers that seemed randomly arranged and its new interior smelled of dried wood. An English pop song, one I had heard long ago but couldn't recall the name of, rolled in waves through the café. We sat by the window. A man with a beard approached us, greeted Soon-mee by name and asked if she wanted coffee. After she had nodded yes, he thrust a small menu at me. I told him that I also wanted coffee.

We sat in awkward silence as we waited. I suddenly felt exhausted. Everything that had happened in Namcheon seemed like it had been a dream. A strange drowsiness surged up in me, and I felt that my eyes were about to close regardless of how hard I tried to keep them open. I dreamed of napping in Soon-mee's arms under the palm tree, and I absurdly imagined that there was some kind of tranquilizer in the music which flowed through the air and into my blood stream.

The bearded waiter returned with our coffee. He told us that he had just made it so it should be really good. Despite his manly appearance, his voice was wispy and soft. His tone made it sound as if he were doing us some huge favor. Maybe because no one else was in the coffee shop, he was almost excessively kind to us. Before leaving our table, he bent over toward Soon-mee and whispered to her, "Would you like to listen to the song?" Looking embarrassed, Soon-mee hurriedly shook her head and this made me believe that the man's over-attentiveness was bothersome. Even after he left, her flushed face didn't immediately return to normal. So I asked her what the man was talking about. But she didn't seem to want to talk about it, saying it was nothing and hastily changing the subject.

"What song was he talking about?" I asked in a louder voice, aiming my question at the waiter, not her. I knew that he would hear me.

"There's a song that she always listens to when she comes in alone," the waiter answered cheerfully, while he placed empty coffee cups in hot water to heat them up.

I didn't understand why she would blush over something like that. Her head still bent, Soon-mee was fidgeting with the handle of her coffee mug. I gazed at her for a moment and then asked the waiter, "Whatever song it is, why don't you play it?"

He seemed to study Soon-mee's reaction but the inside of the coffee shop was too dark for him to see that she was embarrassed. The waiter probably thought the same as I did—that playing a song was no big deal. He wasn't obligated to take music requests from everyone who came into the coffee shop so it was a thoughtful gesture on his part, something he did for special customers. He would certainly not be accused of negligence for overlooking such a detail but his extra-attentiveness would be repaid with gratitude. The man clearly took pride in his service and there weren't any other customers around for him to worry about. He seemed to have decided to do us this favor. After wiping off his wet hands, he walked toward the audio system. Soon the old English pop song stopped and a different song began playing. Leaning her body against the window, Soon-mee lowered her head even further, until it almost reached the table. Listening to the guitar intro to the song, I immediately understood why she was so embarrassed. It was a familiar song. "I gave my heart to you. But here I've stood for such a long time without even a glance from you. How much longer will I stand here waiting for you? Before I melt away, before I melt away, like snow without a trace, take my heart, my photographer . . ."

I knew who the photographer was and who had written the song. But I didn't know how the coffee shop had got hold of it since I had what I thought was the only recording. There must have been other copies. But what was even stranger was that the singer wasn't Soon-mee. And the audio quality was much better than the version I had. Clearly, this was not a home recording. In need of some explanation, I stared at Soon-mee.

She seemed to perceive my silent inquiry. Moving her restless fingers from her coffee cup to her hair, she said in a faint voice, "It was just a coincidence that one day I came in here and happened to hear the song," she said. But this answer didn't satisfy me. She must've known more about it. "In college I gave the song to one of my student friends who was a good singer," she said timidly, as if she had done something wrong, "and she used it in a university song contest and won second place. And I later heard that the song was on the contest album, and one day when I came in here, it was playing."

She must've been surprised and asked the waiter to show her the album. And she must've asked him to play the song again. Maybe she even told him that she had composed it. And so, from then on whenever she came in to the coffee shop the waiter played the song, "Take My Heart My Photographer," as a favor to her, knowing nothing about who the photographer was. The waiter was probably oblivious to the meaning that the song held for Soon-mee and he couldn't have the foggiest idea about the memories she recalled while listening to it.

I was jealous of the photographer who still occupied her heart. Ever since I had secretly listened to her song when I was twenty-one, I'd wished to have her sing to me and only me. It was a hopeless desire and I understood this, but my lingering attachment to the idea would swell up whenever it got the chance; I couldn't do anything about it. I was once again awed by the mysterious workings of human emotions.

"The photographer doesn't take photos any longer," I said jokingly, in an attempt to distract myself from the shame of still being so attached to her.

"I know that and that's why . . ." she immediately responded, as if she had been waiting for me to talk about my brother. I sensed that she had touched on something that wasn't easy for her to express and so she wanted to do it as quickly as possible. She then asked me, "Do you think your brother will take up photography again if he sees me?"

I felt a sudden pang. It was exactly what I had hoped for, but I was still heartbroken. Her attitude was very different from the last time we had met. It was true that I believed she was the only person who could get him to resume photography. However, I began to see that reaching out to her may have had more to do with my yearning to see her again than the ostensible motive of getting my brother to take photos again. Maybe I'd avoided reflecting on my underlying aims because I was afraid of discovering the truth: that I had not sought out Soon-mee based on an altruistic desire to help my brother. Maybe the action was indeed driven by my blind desire to see Soon-mee again, but I also firmly believed that my brother would be saved once I found her. But would he really take up photography again if he saw her? Her question awakened doubts as to whether it would really happen. Suddenly, I felt that ten or more years had passed since we'd returned from Namcheon. To be certain, the place had some surreal quality which made it difficult to distinguish time. But did time flow more slowly there, did it circle back on itself, or was it simply holding its breath?

"Take me to your brother," she said, softly. As she spoke these words the song's refrain began repeating: "Take my heart my photographer, take my heart my photographer ..." Unthinkingly, I sang along with the lyrics. My mind was racing.

"Let me be the woman in his hotel room," she said.

The shocking request froze the song's lyrics in my throat. For a moment I doubted what I had just heard. Right then, the song ended. I raised my eyebrows in disbelief and asked her what she was talking about. She repeated her request, this time more forcefully, determined for me to clearly understand what she wanted to do. Her voice trembled as she spat out the last words "in his hotel room." It was like she was spitting on herself, like she wanted to debase herself. She repeated the words again, adding, "I'm a whore, I'm no different from a whore."

Shocked, I didn't know how to respond. Indecipherable words sputtered out as my heart beat faster and faster. Embarrassed, I called out for refills of coffee. But her coffee cup was still untouched and mine was more than halfway full.

26

"It's true," Soon-mee said, "I'm a whore, I'm no different from a whore." I begged her to stop repeating such nonsense, not out of concern for her, but because I couldn't stand hearing it. But she didn't listen to me. She continued to mercilessly insult herself. She believed that she was a whore just like the women in my brother's hotel room. She could only think this way if she truly loathed herself. I told her that I refused to do what she wanted, but she insisted, claiming that I had an obligation to do it since I had come to her and told her about my brother. She also said that it was my responsibility because I had helped her see who she really was; she said I had helped her realize that she was a worthless whore. But she couldn't convince me. I had never had anything but the highest opinion of her and I couldn't stand to hear her insult herself in this way.

I told her I would arrange a meeting with my brother. It was originally what I had wanted her to do anyway. But her showing up when he expected a prostitute wasn't what I'd had in mind. It didn't suit Soon-mee and, above all, it wasn't what my brother would want. It wouldn't be good for either one of them. But my words were useless. She held fast to her decision. I worried that her sick self-image would lead her down a dangerous path. I felt like I might go crazy if I sat there listening to her say these things any longer, so I got up. The waiter came over with more coffee and stood next to us, looking at our faces in turn, quizzically. A different song was now playing but it didn't seem to mingle with the atmosphere; it was gaudy and generic like thick makeup on an old prostitute's face. At that moment I finally noticed that Soon-mee was crying. Looking at her, I tensed up. I saw that she was seized with guilt and self-loathing, feelings that I wasn't sure that I could empathize with.

"After Woo-hyeon left I lived a wild life," Soon-mee said gloomily, after I'd sat back down again. "I'm not saying I lived that way because of him. I'm just telling you what happened to me and how things have become meaningless since then," she said.

I hadn't told her that I had spied on her or that I had seen her with her elder sister's husband. All I had asked was if her brother-in-law had been the person from the Intelligence Agency who'd given her the false information about my brother. She had seemed embarrassed by my question, which must have been pointed enough to make her feel guilty. At the time I had felt proud of my shrewd detective work but it hadn't been my intention to blame her or to pressure her into divulging any details about the matter.

"I met with my brother-in-law," she said.

"When?" I asked. This word just flew out of my mouth and I was afraid that it might've sounded too eager. Luckily, she didn't seem to take it that way.

"It was after you came to the library to see me. I asked him what had really happened to your brother." Soon-mee confirmed that her source in the Intelligence Agency was indeed her elder sister's husband. He was the person who'd supplied her with bogus information. "I asked him what had really happened and why he'd done that, I mean why he'd lied to me . . . but at first he denied it. So I told him you had come to the library and told me everything . . . and . . ." She went on to tell me that he then offered her an excuse, telling her that he'd had to lie, for her sake. He said that he couldn't tolerate his sister-in-law having a relationship with a crippled man; he just couldn't let her ruin her life.

"What a good brother-in-law," I said. And I was sure that she understood my sarcastic tone. I was insinuating that the person who'd ruined her life was not my brother but her brother-in-law, and I felt that she believed this too. I had to fight my urge to tell her what I'd seen that night on the roof across from her apartment. And she seemed to be struggling over whether to tell me about her relationship with her sister's husband. Finally, she sipped her coffee; she seemed to be trying to calm herself down.

"What was more outrageous," said Soon-mee, after putting her coffee cup back on the table, "was that he met your mother."

"Why my mother?" I asked her. "Why would he need to see my mother? What did he want from her?"

"He said that he was the one who'd made up the stories that your mother told me and he'd forced her to tell me all those lies. He threatened your mother, telling her that it wouldn't be pretty if she didn't do what he wanted. That's why all the information your mother gave me was exactly what he told me later." Soon-mee was short of breath.

I wondered if she was aware of the tone of voice she used when she spoke of her brother-in-law. Whether conscious of it or not, she was revealing her relationship with him. It was clear that he wasn't just her brother-in-law. But I couldn't bring that up now.

"Why did he do all that?" I asked.

She answered immediately, "He's a ruthless man ... he gets whatever he wants," she said. She had answered my question, but only indirectly. I had been suspicious of him from the beginning and Soon-mee now confirmed his character. To me the man was a bastard, period. Not only because he had humiliated me. I no longer cared about what he had done to me. But when she said "he gets whatever he wants" the emotion in her voice made it clear that he had inflicted much pain on her.

Right then the song "Take My Heart My Photographer" began playing again. The coffee shop owner was kind but not very observant. Soon-mee's eyes were brimming with tears and she became silent. The sunlight streamed through the thin curtains. Like day-flies, dust particles danced in the air. And the song's slow and melancholic tempo permeated everything. Soon-mee remained speechless as the song came to an end. I was afraid that the simple-minded waiter would play the song another time, but fortunately, five young women came into the coffee shop. I could bear their raucous chattering if it meant our well-intentioned waiter didn't have time to do us any more favors.

After slurping down my cold coffee, I asked Soon-mee, "Is he the reason? Is your brother-in-law the reason you call yourself a whore and you think you should prostitute yourself for my brother?" I raised my voice on purpose, hoping she would see the absurdity of her reasoning. She didn't answer my question. Her face showed that she was in pain but I didn't let myself be swayed. Again, I flatly refused her request. I explained that the visit to the motel that I took once a month with my brother was more of a medical treatment, like preventive therapy, and that neither of us enjoyed it. I had only explained everything to her so that she would see how much my brother needed her help but that my brother would be deeply ashamed if he knew I had told her. I told her that what she wanted to do for my brother wouldn't be good for anyone, especially my brother, who would be mortified by her self-debasement. It wasn't the right way, and I pleaded with her to stop speaking such nonsense.

Quietly, she listened to me and finally rested her head on the table and began crying. "What can I do, what can I do now . . ." she sobbed.

I imagined putting my hands on her heaving shoulders but I kept them under the table. My clenched palms were wet with sweat which I wiped away on my trousers. Like some kind of sign, the song was playing again: "I gave my heart to you. But here I've stood for such a long time without even a glance from you. How much longer will I stand here waiting for you? Before I melt away, before I melt away, like snow without a trace, take my heart, my photographer . . ."

27

I wasn't sure I had done the right thing by telling Soon-mee about my brother's visits to the motels. I didn't think that it was something I had to hide or be ashamed of but it was still something that I questioned. I once read that the circumstances of a particular situation dictate what's right or wrong and that everything beyond the situation has nothing to do with the truth. The book also said that if an act is motivated by love then the act is good. I interpreted this to mean: if the motive behind an action isn't love then the act is not good. I used to doubt the logic that said even a harmful act was good if motivated by love and a good act was bad if it wasn't motivated by love. But I don't question it any longer. I now accepted the Situationists' argument as an absolute truth. It's as if this argument had been made for my sake. If love is the motive, anything is pardonable. And this was because love is the ultimate goal in all situations and in all matters.

It was difficult to leave Soon-mee after seeing her weeping with her head on the table, saying, "What can I do, what can I do now . . ." Her words echoed in my ears, again and again. As she sat sobbing I realized that I was the only person who could protect Soon-mee. Wiping my sweaty palms against my pants, I pledged to myself, *I will protect this woman.* After Soon-mee and I parted, I repeated those words as I walked alone on the street. The sunbeams through the trees clung to my face like spider webs as I told myself that if this task was my duty, then I would die defending her. Strange, but I had never before felt as close to Soon-mee as when she sat there weeping.

But I wasn't sure how to protect her. After our meeting at the coffee shop, she returned to the library and I walked to a terminal to catch a bus home. Her words "What can I do?" were so clear in my mind that I even turned around to see if she was there. I understood the depths of the abyss she had fallen into. And I wanted to rescue her. *Can I do it?* I asked myself. The face of her sister's husband swam into my mind. It was that bastard's fault. He was the reason Soon-mee thought so poorly of herself. I felt a burning hatred for him. And Soon-mee wasn't the only person whose life was messed up because of him. First of all my brother had been affected by his actions. And next, I thought of my mother, so proud of her "first child." She'd had to endure first her son's devastating injury and then that bastard had forced her to lie to the woman who loved him. And lastly, I recalled the humiliation I suffered because of him. Thinking of all this, my hatred felt as if it would burst out of my skin. I kicked one of trees lining the street. I wanted him to experience my hatred. I hated him as much as I loved Soon-mee. It was as if I could confirm my love for her through my hatred of him. Like an incantation, I recited to myself that my hatred, as a source of love, was beautiful, pure, and sacred. I was aware that I was walking a steep and slippery slope. But when no other path exists, there's only one way to go.

I decided to gather some information about him. It was one of my specialties. I had recorded his license plate number so it wasn't difficult to do. I easily got his name, address, and phone number through one of my former co-workers at The Runners. Then, without hesitation, I called his home.

A woman answered. Her voice somewhat resembled Soon-mee's and so I reckoned she was Soon-mee's elder sister. I told her that I wanted to talk to Mr. Jang Young-dal. She asked me who I was. I gave her a made up name and position — Deputy Manager, Jeong. As I've said before, I learned this trick when working for The Runners — to present some vague job title without giving the name of any organization. Of course, in that case one should be prepared to answer further questions, such as "Deputy Manager, where?" But most housewives usually drop their suspicion once they hear a job title and they don't ask any more questions. It's true, too, that most women in this country have little knowledge of their husbands' life in the outside world.

But this woman wasn't one of them. "Pardon me, but could I ask the reason for your call?" she asked.

At least she was courteous, I thought. "I have something I would like to talk to Mr. Jang about but I only have his home phone number on me. And I'm away from my office right now." These lies came easily to me in the spur of the moment.

"Call his office then, please," she said before hanging up. The phone disconnected with a click. I was in the middle of repeating that I'd called his home because I didn't have his office number, but my words were trapped in the phone line.

Glaring at the receiver, I wondered whether she knew about the relationship between her husband and her younger sister. The short phone conversation I'd had with her didn't reveal anything. I wanted to know how much she knew, but at the same time, I didn't want to let commonplace curiosity distract me from my pure, beautiful, and sacred hatred — so I restrained myself. What I wanted was to maintain my hatred intact, just the way it was. I knew I could easily find out the location of the bastard's office by calling Soon-mee, but I didn't.

That night I walked to Soon-mee's apartment complex. I was a slave to my hatred. It was not only beautiful and pure and sacred but wise as well. I was willing to follow it wherever it led me. Once I read in my mother's Bible that one needs to be as pure as a dove and as wise as a snake. At that time I had difficulty understanding how such contrasting images could converge. What was hard to understand wasn't the juxtaposition of "pure and wise" but the conflicting images of "dove and snake." But now the images represented my belief that my hatred was holy. As if the sentence had been written to explain my feelings, I felt camaraderie with the words, and reciting them made me happy. Purity and wisdom, dove and snake.

I returned to the roof of the commercial building in front of Soon-mee's apartment complex. I tried to justify my behavior by telling myself that this was the only way for me to protect her, but this rationalization didn't stop me from feeling that my dignity was diminished, wrinkled like crumpled linen trousers. With a can of beer in hand I leaned against the railing. Soon-mee arrived home late that night. By then, I had emptied two beers. I was slightly concerned about her returning so late. But when I saw her sister's husband accompanying her I became furious. Not knowing how to deal with my inexplicable sense of betrayal and anger, I began to pace the roof of the building. I cursed the force of my hatred which had brought me back to the roof of this building. I felt like an animal confined to a cage. At one point I even growled like a beast.

Sitting on the sofa, Soon-mee's brother-in-law immediately turned on the TV. By coincidence, a commercial for the beer I was drinking appeared on the screen. This was followed by an ad for a se-curities investment company, which he seemed to dislike and so he changed the channel. Baseball players appeared on a green field, but he soon switched to a soccer game. Looking like he'd finally found something he liked, he placed the remote control on the table.

Meanwhile, Soon-mee moved through the apartment. She went into her bedroom and came out wearing different clothes and then she went into the bathroom and came out with a towel around her head, and then to the kitchen, to the veranda, back to the kitchen, to the living room, and back again to the kitchen. I watched their every move, now and then leaning against the railing to get a better look. Depending on my position relative to her window, the scene inside her apartment played out either as a single frame or a split screen. I was disappointed in her and enraged by him. I wished I could change the channel and dispel the scene. My emotions were jumbled inside me; a human being's psyche is too complex to be easily understood.

As I continued watching them I was surprised by what I saw. What I had expected was that their bodies would soon meet and the curtain would be drawn. And then her lights would be turned off. I was prepared for all that. But contrary to my expectation their bodies didn't meet nor were the curtains drawn. And the lights weren't turned off either. Instead, they both stood glaring at each other, apparently having a tense conversation. Soon he vio-lently smacked the back of Soon-mee's neck. Falling to the floor, she covered her head with her hands. He then kicked her, shouting, but I couldn't make out his words. I felt my heart pounding in my temples. *He shouldn't have done that. No one has the right to do that to her*, I thought. *That bastard should never ever be allowed to hurt her again.* I clenched my teeth, determined that no one would ever again do such a thing to her in front of me. He now held her by her hair and with his other hand he punched her repeatedly in the face, arms, bosom, and stomach. And she didn't resist his blows. She just lay weeping on the floor. I couldn't hear her, but I knew for sure that she was crying. My heart heard everything clearly and it was telling me to act. I felt humiliated for her, and I felt her pain. I couldn't just stand there watching.

I took out my cell phone and dialed her number. Her phone must've been ringing, but the scene didn't change. The man was still beating her, performing his role in the scene, and the woman was enacting her part as the defenseless victim of violence. Frantic, I began shouting, "Pick up the phone! Please, answer it . . ." But they seemed not to notice the ringing. They were too engrossed in their real-life drama. Hurling my unfinished can of beer away, I dashed down the stairs. I didn't have any idea what I was going to do but I had to find a way to save her from that bastard.

Reaching the door to her apartment, I repeatedly rang the bell. I then pounded the metal door with my fist, shouting, "Is anybody home?"

"Who's there?" the bastard yelled out. His voice conveyed his irritation at the late night intruder. It wasn't likely that he would open the door. I hurriedly told him that I was the building's security guard and that there was a fire in the apartment below, so everyone had to quickly evacuate the building.

"What's all this stupidity?" he complained, but his anger had noticeably diminished. As for me, I would've done anything to stop what was happening inside, even if I had to set fire to the building.

"Evacuate, quickly evacuate," I shouted my lines like a good actor. My pride in my acting ability convinced me that he would open the door. Anxiously glaring at the sad gray door as I waited for it to open, my fury began to increase. I conjured up hatred, hatred as the origin of love and as the other face of love, hatred so chaste and pure and sacred and wise. And this hatred of mine was about to erupt. I would've done anything to protect Soon-mee. Anything.

Just as I was about to explode, the dreary metal door finally opened halfway and the man stuck his face out. Immediately, I realized how uncontrollable rage can be. It burst out through my muscles, the muscles of my arms and fists, muscles hardened by hatred. As I pummeled him with blows from my iron fists, blows to his face, chest, and abdomen, I thought that I might be capable of killing the bastard. But I continued beating him; I didn't care what happened.

28

Soon-mee was crying. It was almost as if only through tears could her soul express itself. Without thinking about what I was doing, I dragged her out of her apartment and put her into the car. Before I got in, I searched for the bastard's brown car and when I found it I punctured all the tires. But this didn't appease my anger, so I pulled out a bar of the metal fence along the flowerbeds and smashed his car's windshield, again and again. I watched as the glass fractured into patterns like a thousand spider webs. From the other side of the darkness, the security guard began running toward me, shouting. I ran back to Soon-mee, started the car, and sped out of the parking lot. In an instant we were gone.

The world was dark; it seemed that not a single streetlight was lit. I sped along the road, not knowing where I was going. Any place would have been fine as long as it was far from Soon-mee's brother-in-law. Soon-mee was still crying and I also noticed that she was now shaking uncontrollably. I couldn't stand to see her trembling. "Please, calm down," I yelled, realizing that I was also trembling. We were both shaking with fear. Cutting through the darkness, thick as a black curtain, the car raced ahead like a fighter plane on a mission to detonate a ticking time bomb. And maybe it was true. I imagined my body as a bombshell loaded with explosives ready to detonate. I probably held a secret wish to blow up my car with Soon-mee and me in it.

Soon-mee continued shaking and sobbing as I slammed down on the accelerator and shouted, "What were you thinking? Don't you know he's a rotten bastard? Don't you see that he's been damaging you, mentally and physically, destroying your soul? Are you that dumb? Why do you have to do this? Why him of all men? I don't understand. I just don't understand why you don't defend yourself and why you're throwing yourself away like that. He's a demon! That bastard is a demon, understand?"

But she kept crying. It was as if she had forgotten all other forms of communication, like a baby who doesn't have any other way to express itself. Overwhelmed by pity for her, I almost started crying myself. But I managed to gain control of my emotions.

"Don't worry. You don't need to worry—I'll protect you from now on. I can't bear to see you suffer and I won't forgive anyone who hurts you. So please, don't worry. I'm here now." I said this solemnly, as if trying to convince myself. But her crying became even louder. Tears suddenly welled up in my eyes. Was I touched by my own words? They sounded convincing enough but deep down I didn't believe what I had said. A wide ravine lay between my resolution and my reality. Emotionally charged and unsure of what to do, I just kept talking as she kept crying. I had felt a passionate conviction when I shouted that her lover was a demon but when I swore that I would always protect her, my heart sank, knowing it was a lie.

"Where am I going?" Roads converged into new ones. The car tore through the night air on the unfamiliar roads. We soon entered a major highway but I continued to drive recklessly. Cars scattered to make way for me. Some drivers came to a screeching halt while others honked and shouted. But none of those sounds stopped me. There were probably calls made to the police informing them of an out of control vehicle. But no police car appeared behind me. I wouldn't have cared anyway. I had more important things on my mind.

I sped along the highway until dawn and thanks only to the defensive driving of others, we didn't have an accident. I eventually exited the highway. By then Soon-mee had cried herself to sleep, tear stains still streaking her cheeks. And as the eastern sky began blushing pink, the car ran out of gas on a remote road. After the all-night speeding frenzy, the car was also exhausted and needed to rest.

I felt empty, as if something that had inflated inside me had suddenly burst and was leaking out. Resting my head against the driver's seat, I closed my eyes. Things that had happened only several hours before seemed now like ancient history. It felt like it had all been a dream. Several hours seemed like several hundred years as we'd spent an eternity speeding between different lives.

I opened my eyes and lifted my head to look at Soon-mee beside me. The face of the woman I loved was finally within reach. She looked to be completely at peace and it seemed to me at that moment that she trusted me absolutely. I felt like I was dreaming. I couldn't believe that I was sitting so close to her, gazing into her untroubled face. I wanted to touch her cheeks, to wipe away the stains with my hands. But I felt that if I touched her it would snap me out of my beautiful dream. Instead, I withdrew my hands, which had momentarily hovered above her face. I then softly leaned my head against hers and closed my eyes. I felt her gentle breathing. It was bliss. I felt I could happily face the end of the world like that. I didn't want to think about anything else.

29

"I had a dream," Soon-mee said.

Before I had fallen asleep I had decided I would remain with my head resting on hers until the world ended. I had slept shallowly next to Soon-mee who tossed and turned but feeling her gentle breath on my skin, I was transported to a sweet fantasy world. I allowed myself to imagine that I had finally earned her love and she was now my woman, something I had given up as hopeless. But the daydream had to end. Soon-mee moved again and I opened my eyes. This time she lifted her head from the headrest and sat up, looking around.

The curving road in front of us stretched into the distance and snaked up into the far away mountains. Soon-mee's gaze followed the quiet road through the foothills. The scene was peaceful. But then the specks on the windshield reminded me of the previous night's madness: wings and fragments of insects completely coated the glass. I hadn't been worried about the bugs as I'd sped along, the car slamming into their tiny bodies that filled the air. The sunlight glistened on their delicate wings. Now and then cars passed us on the road.

"I had a strange dream," Soon-mee said, softly. She didn't look like she had fully awoken; rather, it seemed that she had pulled her dream out of her sleep and was still experiencing it. Even though she had just woken up, her face was clear and radiant. There almost seemed to be a halo around her as the sun coming in through the window hit the side of her face.

Suppressing my desire to press my lips against her cheek, I asked her, "What was the dream about?"

"It was strange," she answered. It sounded again as if she were still dreaming. "Was it about me? There was a woman in my dream who was me at one moment and then another person the next and this person changed back into me, and back and forth. And I'm still not sure if it was me," Soon-mee said. "There was a man and a woman who live in the village of a medieval manor. They love each other," she continued. "The man is a bugle player. With his bugle, he lets people know when to get up, when to begin working, when to stop working, and when to go to bed. And so the events of their daily lives are orchestrated by his bugle. The woman is a maiden from a respected family. The bugler loves the woman, who is charming and beautiful. She also loves the man as much as he loves her. So they're happy together. At night the bugler lulls all the dwellers of the manor to sleep, and afterwards, he goes to his lover. Every night, under the stars, they pledge their love to each other. Since the stars are so numerous, their pledges of love are also numerous. But suddenly, a black cloud appears. The lord of the manor desires her. He asks for her hand. And, of course, she refuses. She says, 'I already love another.' But the lord continues pursuing her. And she continues to refuse him. 'No, I love someone else,' she says. So the lord commands her father, his subject, to change his daughter's mind. And her father tries to persuade her, wondering why she doesn't comply with the lord's wishes. He explains that if she becomes his wife, the manor will be hers. But she shakes her head, saying that she already loves someone else. So her father finally gives up. But the lord doesn't."

Right then, a huge truck, packed with freight, zipped by, honking loudly and causing the car to shake. I knew that the truck driver was warning me about stopping on a road without a shoulder, but my car was out of gas. I put on the emergency blinkers. I had known that we were low on fuel before the car died but I never noticed when the fuel light came on in the early morning. I had no idea where we were now.

"It sounds like a fairy tale," I told her. I had been a little nervous about what she might have dreamed after the night we'd had. It was a strange dream, as she'd said, but it didn't sound ominous.

"A fairy tale?" she said with a weary smile.

"Why . . . don't you think so?" I asked, smiling brightly to lift her spirits.

She didn't respond. Instead, she sighed and opened the window. "Where are we?" she asked, inhaling deeply.

I told her that I didn't know. She turned her head and looked at me. "We drove all night and ran out of gas." I explained, forcing an awkward smile. But she wasn't smiling. Trying to lighten the mood and not knowing what to do next, I asked Soon-mee to finish the story. "What happened after that? You left off where the woman's father gave up trying to change her mind but the lord didn't give up."

"Do you want to hear more?" she asked. I nodded. So she resumed her story. "The manor's lord was persistent and stubborn. He would do anything to get what he wanted and his wishes had never been thwarted." As she spoke, I sensed a sadness in her voice. "The lord soon learns that the man whom the woman loves so much is a commoner, a mere bugler. His pride hurt, the lord takes the bugle away from him. He then gives him a lance instead and sends him off to war. The war is severe and brutal. The woman's lover has only blown his bugle for most of his life and so he doesn't even know how to use his lance in battle. He soon loses his eyes and arms in the war. He returns home maimed, but the woman still loves him regardless of his deformity. But the bugler suffers for her. He wants her to stop loving him. He shouts, 'How could you love me, a man with no arms and no eyes. Your love is a torture to me. So leave, please leave!' But she shakes her head, saying she refuses. 'Don't you remember our pledge to the stars?' she tells him. 'If all the stars in the sky disappear, only then will I stop loving you. But as long as the stars shine, my love will also shine. Remember, wherever you go, I'll be with you.'

So the bugler goes to the god of the sea and, standing at the seashore, he pleads to the god, 'Please take me from my love. Send me somewhere far away so she won't be able to find me.' He then jumps into the water. The god sympathizes with his sadness and is touched by his deep love, a love that forces him to abandon his beloved. So the god turns him into a bugle-shaped seed and lets it flow away. The seed travels across the ocean. After some time has passed, a tree begins to grow on the opposite shore. The tree rises toward the sky, wanting to reach the stars, the stars by which the bugler and his lover had once pledged their love. At night the tree plays music, like a bugle. And this music travels across the ocean. After the bugler disappeared, the woman could neither eat nor sleep and she became emaciated. But one day she hears the familiar bugle sounds and runs to the ocean. She knows the sounds are coming from her lover. Weeping, she pleads to the god of the sea, 'Please let me cross the ocean. My love is calling me from the other shore. Take me there, please.' But the god shakes his head. He can't break his promise to the ill-fated bugler who lost his arms and eyes. The god is sad for her but he ignores her crying pleas in order to keep his promise. The woman continues to beseech the god of the sea but he doesn't even respond to her. She vows never to leave the seashore and soon becomes sick and weak from lack of sleep and food. Dehydrated like a mummy, she finally collapses and dies."

Soon-mee rolled down the car window a bit more, as if she needed to feel the outside air. Through the open window, the sun beamed into the car. And the dayflies' wings shone like silver, reminding me of the ocean glistening in the morning sun. I picked up the smell of salt water in the breeze and it occurred to me that the ocean might be nearby.

It was obvious that Soon-mee's dream wasn't just a fairytale. And she was right when she said that it was strange. Soon, her unstable emotions seemed to transfer to me; my nerves felt electrified. I knew something that she didn't. I knew why her dream felt so real, like something she had lived before or a premonition of something yet to come. I was the only one who could correctly interpret her dream. I was there to fit all the pieces together. I was saddened by the realization that I would have to content myself with being a mere interpreter of Soon-mee's dreams; I would always be an outsider and never a player in her dreams. My face burned as I felt my inadequacy, as if I had been clothed in rags before royalty. But Soon-mee hadn't finished recounting her dream.

After a moment had passed, she continued. "The maiden's death stirred the god of the sea who had been unmoved by her pleas. The god now regretted his unsympathetic response. And so, he turned her into a seed as well. Soon a tree rose at the spot where she had died. The tree grew rapidly toward the sky, eager to reach the stars, the stars that the woman and her lover had pledged their love to. Now two tall trees stand at opposite sides of the ocean, linking earth and sky. They're poised, ready to race toward each other. But trees aren't able to race, nor can they fly. They're rooted and immobile. Their love still seems hopeless, even after they've been transformed into trees. But it's not the end of the story. The last part of the dream is mysterious and bizarre. Every night, the time that they had always spent together making their pledges of love to the stars, the trees' roots move at an incredible speed. All the trees' energy is concentrated in their roots which race quickly through the soil under the ocean water. Yes, every night the roots of each tree race toward the opposite shore of the ocean. They join midway and intertwine. Like the hands of lovers, their roots reach out to caress each other and join in a tight embrace.

"What a strange dream, but such a vivid one. It was so clear and detailed, almost as if I had really lived it. And while I dreamed, I felt someone touching my face. Was the woman me? What does this dream mean?"

When she finished recounting her dream, I was struck by its familiar ending. I recalled driving back to Seoul after the funeral in Namcheon hounded by wild images of the palm tree. I had imagined the tree's roots reaching the ocean and the ocean hugging the tree. And I remembered saying, no, it was the opposite—the tree hugged the ocean. And the tree's roots reached across the waters. I imagined the tree's deep, long roots crossing the Pacific and reaching the coasts of Brazil or Indonesia. And I even thought that maybe the tree's roots traveled across the ocean nightly. I also thought then that it was the most unfair prejudice to think that trees are immobile. I remember uttering to myself that if a tree can travel to Namcheon it should also be able to travel back and I was convinced that trees actually move; we just can't see it. But my daydream about the tree had been incomplete because I never considered why the tree had crossed the ocean. I was even so egocentric as to think that Soon-mee had had her dream just to complete my daydream.

"All trees are incarnations of frustrated love." This sentence, as if it had been on standby, suddenly flashed across my mind. It seemed to come out of nowhere. But as I uttered these words, I remembered their source. It was my brother who had written this line. I had read the sentence in a notebook that I had found in his room a long time ago. He had written over two hundred pages about the myths in which fairies often disguised themselves as trees in order to avoid the gods' lust and greed. The gods are the ones who possess power, and those with power are always ravenous. Their gluttony cannot be curbed. The only way for fairies to escape the destructive greed of the gods is to transform into trees. And that's why each tree has its own sad and unfulfilled love story. He also had written down many stories about the origins of specific flowers and trees.

I had wondered then why my brother wrote about such things. Maybe he was just passing the time, but it seemed so odd to collect myths about trees for fun. Later, after he had been injured, I hoped that he had kept up his writing since an interest in something, anything, would be good for his mental health. When I saw that the pine tree and the snowbell at the end of the forest path aroused such zeal in him, I was again reminded of those writings and I concluded that my brother must be obsessively infatuated with nature.

But how could I explain Soon-mee's dream, which sounded like it had come straight out of my brother's writing or my own daydream? She said that it had been very realistic and detailed, but in actuality, it was nothing but a myth. My usual way of thinking had changed lately; I had become more superstitious. The bugler in Soon-mee's dream reminded me of my brother. *Maybe he wanted them both to become trees and he projected his wish into her dream. But how? Has she read his writing? Could my brother control Soon-mee's dreams? Could he actually enter her dreams while I just roamed around outside them?* This last thought made me again feel utterly insignificant next to my brother and Soon-mee's deep soul connection. "He directs her dreams and I just interpret them. This is the reason for my existence," I muttered to myself.

"Did you say something?" she asked.

"Was it a palm tree?" I asked her.

"I'm sorry, what did you say?" she asked.

I hesitated for a moment, but I soon managed to explain, "I was thinking about your dream." Her clear, beautiful eyes reflected the sunlight. My emotions surged, but I held back my tears. In an attempt to stem them, I squinted. "I meant the tree in your dream, was it a palm tree?" I asked again. I wanted to confirm a hunch.

"How did you know that?" she asked, her eyes wide with surprise.

This confirmation cleared away all my lingering doubts; I was now resigned to my allotted role in relation to Soon-mee. The feeling that my place had been dictated by some unknown power helped me surrender. I didn't think that my brother controlled this power but I wasn't absolutely sure that he didn't. I realized that I had to take Soon-mee to the house on top of the cliff in Namcheon where the palm tree stood.

I blankly gazed at what was left of the insect bodies still covering the windshield. I stepped out of the car and tried to clean the glass with my hands. But they didn't come off easily. I then took a rag from the trunk and began to rub them away. "We need to find out where we are and where we can get some gas," I told Soon-mee, while I vigorously rubbed the windshield.

"You really have no idea where we are?" she asked, stepping out of the car.

"Well . . . not yet. Last night I just drove without any sense of direction," I explained. Suddenly, I caught another whiff of saltwater in the air. Putting the rag back into the trunk, I took a closer look at the snaking road drenched in bright sunlight. The far end of the curve skirted the foot of a mountain. "Ah, okay! I knew it looked familiar . . ." I exclaimed. I thought I had driven without any direction or destination in mind, but the fact that I had ended up in this place after a night of mindless driving couldn't possibly be a coincidence. Had my recklessness actually been guided by fate? I knew that if we went around the next curve of the mountain, the ocean and the palm tree would appear. We were in Namcheon.

30

Expecting some kind of miracle, I tried to start the car, but to no avail. I once more glanced at the winding road tapering away toward the foot of the mountain and suggested to Soon-mee that we take a short walk. She asked me where we were going. With a faint smile, I answered that we would be walking into her dream. She looked me in the eye to see if I was joking. I responded to her unspoken question with an expression that showed I wasn't kidding, and she followed behind me along the road.

"Are you sure you know where we're going?" she asked when we arrived at the hilltop where the narrow path began. The ocean had just appeared below us. She looked concerned and I almost laughed at her uneasiness. I nodded my head and started up the mountain path.

"We're almost there . . . it's just around that curve," I told her. The ocean was bathed in silver as shattered pieces of sunlight glistened on the water's surface. I wondered if I needed to tell her about the palm tree on the cliff before we turned the corner. But I didn't know how or where to begin the story. But I decided that I wouldn't need to explain anything. In most cases an explanation isn't even very helpful; only through seeing and experiencing can one truly understand. Everything would become clear to her the moment she saw the tree.

"Oh my god!" she exclaimed. I didn't ask her what she had seen. I didn't need to ask. She was looking at the palm tree. The tree on top of the sheer cliff had to have been the tree she saw in her dream.

"Am I still dreaming?" she asked, gazing down at the ocean unfolding beneath us.

"Who knows, maybe you have stepped back into your dream," I replied.

"How can it be? I can't believe it, how is it . . ." she stammered, too astonished to finish her sentence.

"Either this is a dream now or the dream you had wasn't a dream," I suggested tentatively. My mystical speech sounded ridiculous to me but I continued, "All trees are incarnations of frustrated love." This sentence from my brother's writings had been lingering in my mind. "This place is not of this world. It's the same place that you saw in your dream. The tree is a dream too," I said. The situation seemed so surreal that I wondered for a moment if I were the one dreaming. "But I'm not a protagonist in this dream. I'm outside of it," I hurriedly added. She didn't ask me then who the main characters were. She didn't even look at me. It seemed that she had finally grasped the whole situation, especially the fact that I was an outsider. Even though this was something I'd expected, I still couldn't help feeling rejected.

I reminded myself of my role in this situation. I had searched for Soon-mee, reasoning that my brother needed her, and I had convinced her to see him. Her negative self-image made her believe that the only way she deserved to see him was as a prostitute. I was between them, between my brother, who wanted to become a tree, and Soon-mee, who wanted to become a prostitute. But they shared a common motive for wanting to become something other than what they were: love. Transforming themselves was the only way either of them could imagine for their impossible love to bear fruit. They each longed to be with the other but neither believed that they could be accepted for who they truly were. That's why they could only imagine their love through dreams and myths, in places that didn't exist in this world. My role had been set. And I was determined to do my best.

"That palm tree . . . its seed washed up on the shore about thirty-five years ago. When it reached this spot, after its long journey across the ocean, a man and a woman were staying here. They loved each other but they knew that their love could not survive in the real world. And so they wanted to leave that world. And this was their place of refuge. But their love was thwarted. What grew in this place instead of their love was the seed of the tropical tree they had planted. And you're looking at it. You're looking at the aspirations and dreams that they planted along with the seed. You're looking at their frustrated love, transformed into a tree."

I didn't feel that Soon-mee really needed an explanation. I believed that she could sense the story of the tree just by looking, as if she had a spiritual connection to it. But regardless, I couldn't stop speaking. Maybe I needed to say these things in order to help myself understand. The words I spoke didn't seem to be my own. It was not like me to speak this way about mysterious and illogical ideas. Still amazed, Soon-mee's gaze was fixed on the treetop. She didn't even appear to be listening to me.

"And would you believe that the man and woman had a reunion under that palm tree after a thirty-five-year separation?" I said. "It's unbelievable but true. One of them was old and sick and the other was old but not sick. And fate didn't allow them to share much time together, even after they were finally reunited. The sick man died soon after, as if he had been holding on only for that moment. Hiding right here, I watched their two bodies, naked and unashamed like the first humans, become one under that tree just before the old man died. It was a beautiful and touching scene. But I didn't know why I had experienced it that way until today. If you hadn't told me about your dream, I would've never seen it so clearly. Yes, I'm now certain that they were in a world protected from time, the very force that had kept them apart. And the palm tree was the embodiment of their love and hope. They were in their own sanctum, hidden in the innermost depths of reality, a place that time cannot penetrate. All obstacles, all demands, and all restrictions are absent here. And that's why I was deeply moved."

We stood under the palm tree, its shadow covering us. The wooden platform, where I had seen the two incomplete bodies unite as one whole, was half shaded and vacant. I ran my palm across it. And I felt fine grains of sand. Mindlessly, I kept running my hand across the platform, brushing the sand off before I finally invited Soon-mee to sit down. But she didn't seem to hear me. Speechless, she stood under the palm tree. She seemed overwhelmed by the surreal atmosphere of the place, made all the more surreal by her recent dream. It wasn't that she had entered her dream. This place had been summoned into a dream in which she was perfectly cast as the main character.

31

At a grocery store located nearby, I bought some rice, kimchi, spinach, tofu, and some sliced, frozen fish. I bought some bread and milk and instant curry. I bought toothbrushes and toothpaste and soap and shampoo. I bought two towels and two pairs of socks and skin lotion and facial tissue. I bought a bag of instant coffee and creamer and paper cups and canned fruit juice. The cashier at the store, a young woman, asked me if I was moving into a new home. Instead of answering her, I asked her if there was a gas station nearby.

"Not here but in town. Why?" she asked.

"My car ran out of gas," I told her.

"Oh no, what can we do?" she said, concerned, as if it was her problem. "There's an auto shop nearby, but I don't think they carry gasoline. But who knows, maybe they do. Check it out," she said, and then gave me directions to the shop. Arms laden with grocery bags, I began walking toward the shop.

As the young woman had suspected, the shop didn't have gasoline. The owner first looked me over and then asked, "Why do you need gas?" I repeated the same answer I had given the woman at the grocery store. Wiping his sweaty forehead with his oil-stained shirt sleeve, the man said that he had planned to go to town in a little while to get gasoline anyway and that he would get some for me if I wasn't in a hurry and I could wait.

"My car is on the road at the foot of the mountain. You can't miss it," I told him. I gave him my plate number. The man said that he will drop off a gasoline container next to my car. I then paid him for it.

Soon-mee agreed with my plan, which was to bring my brother to Namcheon and encourage him to take photos of her there. I was glad that she wouldn't be meeting him in a motel room. She wasn't a prostitute and she shouldn't want to become one. And I knew there wasn't any better place for them to meet than Namcheon, under the palm tree, a space that didn't exist in this world and thus couldn't be affected by time. Soon-mee didn't question my plan and I took this to mean that she thought it would work. She even said she'd rather stay there while I returned to Seoul to get my brother. I didn't see any reason why she couldn't do so, but I was concerned about her, a young woman alone out there. She seemed confident that she would be safe and I had to agree that she would probably be better off there than back at her apartment in Seoul. So I'd stocked up on everything she might need. She said that she had no appetite, but I insisted that she eat something. I then began to put away the supplies I had bought.

The house was neat and clean and empty. Since the old man had died, no one had any reason to come here, and his former driver, who had taken care of him until he died, had moved away.

"Are you sure you'll be okay alone?" I again asked Soon-mee. I was still hesitant, even after getting the house ready for her. "Turning her head away from me, she nodded. "I'll be back tomorrow, but if anything happens, the day after tomorrow at the latest, which means you'll be here alone for one or two days. Are you sure you're okay with that?" I asked her once again. I knew that everything was already decided, but I still didn't feel comfortable leaving her behind. It would be dark soon and I was worried about her spending the night alone at such a remote spot. I recalled the pledge I had made to protect her in whatever situation. It felt like such a long time ago, but only one day had passed and I was already about to break my promise.

"Strange . . . but it's so peaceful here. This place feels somehow familiar," she said, softly, without looking at me. She seemed to be feeling sorry about something. I knew that it was time for me to leave, but I still couldn't. And it wasn't just because I was worried about her. My lingering attachment to her was holding me back. It was like I was feeling a sense of loss. Even though I had willingly created this situation, my sadness over losing Soon-mee forever was much greater than I had expected.

"Don't skip a meal. If you don't feel like preparing anything, you can eat out. You'll see a café near the village store if you walk for about twenty minutes along the beach," I told her. I then put on my jacket and shoes.

"Ki-hyeon," she said as I turned to leave.

I'm not absolutely sure, though I'm pretty certain, that it was the first time she had ever directly called me by name. Instantly, I became elated. I turned around.

"Thank you," she said, faintly.

Her voice was barely audible, but I saw her heart expressed in her face. A lump rose in my throat. And my longing for her, which I had been trying to contain, suddenly surged inside me. "Would you please do me a favor?" I asked. Nervously, she blinked her eyes. "Please say yes," I begged. My voice was trembling, I was afraid that she might reject my request. She nodded slightly. I wanted to believe that she had decided to do me a favor, not because of my desperate plea but because of her trust in me.

"Do you know when I first became jealous of my brother? It was when I heard you sing to him in his room. I used to sneak in there when he was out and secretly listen to your songs. I still have one of the tapes that I took from his room. It's entitled, "Soon-mee's Songs for Woo-hyeon." And you have no idea how many times I listened to it while I was away from home. The tape's all worn out now. Whenever I listened to it, my heart yearned for you to sing it for me only. My darling . . . oh, I'm sorry, please forgive me for addressing you like that. But so many times my heart called out for you that way. It was how I expressed my love for you. From the time I first listened to your songs, my dream was to have you sing for me and no one else. Would you sing a song for me? Only for me?" I felt as if I had poured my heart out in one breath. My face burned and sweat rose up on my nose and forehead.

Soon-mee looked like she was about to cry. She seemed uneasy, as if she didn't know what to do. I could accept her refusal. For some reason, though, I was confident that she wouldn't.

After a moment, she said faintly, in a childlike voice, "I don't have my guitar."

"Why do you need your guitar?" I asked her, smiling. The sound of the waves continued to crash against the cliff. It sounded to me like a musical prelude to her song and I hoped that she would interpret the ocean sounds the way I did. She turned toward the water. Her hair blew toward me on the breeze and then retreated back to her.

"What song should I sing?" she mumbled, as if asking herself. But I managed to make out her words.

I immediately asked her to sing "Take My Heart My Photographer." Turning around, she looked at me, her eyes filled with suspicion. "I know you wrote that song for my brother. And I also know that you're filled with love when you sing it. Of course, I've never seen you sing it. But I can feel your heart through your voice. I can feel your emotions and visualize your expressions when I listen to it. Whenever I listened to that song, I could see your face. Please take my heart . . . please sing it for me." And I knew that even though she would be thinking of my brother while singing it, I was ready to accept that.

Facing the ocean, she closed her eyes and leaned against the palm tree. Holding in my mind the image of the tree's shadow wrapped around her body, I closed my eyes. At that moment I existed only to listen to her. All other senses were dulled or withered or submerged. The waves struck the cliff as if accompanying her. I waited. Finally, I heard a faint voice, which seemed to be coming from far away, maybe from the other side of the ocean or from many years in the past. I knew the lyrics and the melody by heart. Even though her voice was faint, I heard the song in all its perfection. "I gave my heart to you. But here I've stood for such a long time without even a glance from you. How much longer will I stand here waiting for you? Before I melt away, before I melt away, like snow without a trace, take my heart, my photographer . . ." Her voice now extended across the ocean and into the long gone past. The sky and earth and sea all held their breath to listen to her song. It took me a moment to realize that I was crying. And she was also crying. I realized then that what I had wanted all along was to have someone sing a song just for me. And this wish of mine had finally come true. My tears were understandable. They were inevitable. But her tears were mysterious. Could it be that she also loved me, if only for that short moment?

32

My cell phone rang as I was approaching Seoul. It was my mother. Her voice sounded urgent and anxious. "Where are you?" she demanded. I asked her if something had happened but Mother, instead of answering my question, only said, "Come home quickly, please hurry." I could tell that she was flustered. So I asked again what had happened. "Your brother . . . he's missing," she said.

This was a total surprise. And I didn't mean just because of my brother's physical limitation. To begin with, he wasn't the kind of person who would leave his home and family. No, not my brother. I was that kind of person. I had left home for quite a long time. But my brother would never leave without a good reason. He was the shining light of my family. My parents didn't even notice when I stayed out all night. Last night was a good example. With Soon-mee in my car, I'd driven until early morning and finally stopped in Namcheon, but Mother wasn't alarmed and didn't even ask me where I had spent the night. Well, it wasn't my parents' fault. They were accustomed to my ways. And there was a chance that they weren't even aware of my absence. But my brother was a different case. If I vanished, it wouldn't disturb anything. But my brother's disappearing would. That's why I couldn't believe he was gone. And in his condition, I couldn't think of any place he could've possibly gone alone.

"What are you saying?" I pressed Mother for more information.

"I don't know . . . he was home until dusk . . . we've been looking for him . . . there aren't many places he could've gone to . . . I have this uneasy feeling . . ." Mother said.

I told her that I'd be home soon and hung up. It was already well past dark. The clock on the dashboard read 8:40. The words "uneasy feeling" alarmed me. I sped up and began to pass the other cars on the road.

Mother was restlessly pacing in front of the doorway when I arrived home. Seeing me, she broke into tears. "It's all my fault, my fault. I thought he was okay now … I didn't notice anything unusual, so I thought he had adjusted to things, but I was wrong. All of it must've been too much of a shock for him. It's my fault, isn't it? What should I do? I can't think of any other place he could've possibly gone … where is he? Do you have any idea?" This reaction was as out of the ordinary as my brother's disappearance, since Mother was always calm and cool, almost cold. I could see the degree of her fear. She was riddled with guilt, believing she had caused his disappearance. It seemed to me that the guilty feelings were her own creation, with little or no relationship to reality.

"Your father went to the Lotus Flower Market. I thought your brother might have gone there, so I asked him to go," Mother told me.

"Did Woo-hyeon have any trouble before he disappeared?" I asked her. What I meant was whether my brother had had a fit while I was gone.

Mother nodded and said, "Yes, he had a fit today … I heard him … the maid said that after the fit, he didn't come out of his room. She said he must've been in there the entire afternoon, since she didn't see him leave. But when she called him to dinner she didn't get any response. So she opened his door, but he wasn't in his room. Where did he go? Where? And I don't know why your father hasn't called yet … what's he doing?" Nervously, Mother paced about.

I told her that I didn't think it was likely that my brother had gone to the Lotus Flower Market since he wouldn't need to go there to see a woman after having a fit, maybe before, like the doctor said, but not after.

"That makes sense, but who knows what's on his mind," Mother said. Her voice revealed her impatience. She suggested that maybe we should check the motels on the outskirts of the city, just in case, but this only confirmed that she was panicking. I sympathized with her but at the same time I knew that so much anxiety and fear wasn't doing any good.

"Maybe he needed some fresh air. Or who knows, maybe he had something to do downtown, and since no one was around to help him, he went on his own. I'm sure he'll be back soon. Don't worry," I told Mother. I said this in order to help ease her anxiety, but it didn't mean I wasn't apprehensive. I remembered my brother's self-loathing, something he had plainly revealed in the car on the way home from trips to the motel or after having a fit, and this increased my concern. Recently, he had been even more taciturn, rarely speaking at all. Since I had no idea what went on in his head, I was always concerned about him. No one could be completely sure that he wouldn't do something extreme. I asked Mother if she had searched his room. If he had left home with some intention in mind, some hint of it may've been left behind.

"I did check, but I didn't see anything unusual," Mother answered.

I walked into my brother's room and guided by intuition, I went straight to his desk drawer. The collection of his writings wasn't there but in the drawer was a manila envelope. As if I had driven from Namcheon solely for this reason, I opened the envelope without any hesitation. It was a manuscript. I knew the stories from memory: one story was about the fairy Daphne who turned into a bay tree in order to avoid Apollo. "The free-spirited and attractive Daphne appealed to her father, the god of rivers, to help her escape from Apollo, who was pursuing her. 'Please change my appearance!' she pleaded. 'Take this beautiful body away from me, this body that brings me such suffering!' So her father turned her into a bay tree." Another story was about Pitys who was loved by the god Pan. "Both Pan and Boreas loved Pitys. Boreas was the god of the north wind. Learning that Pitys loved Pan more than him, Boreas was seized with jealousy and blew her off a cliff. Discovering the dying Pitys, Pan turned her into a pine tree." There was a story about a lovesick woman who through a misunderstanding was turned into an almond tree. "Phyllis, the princess of Thrace, waited for her lover who had gone off to the Trojan War. But when her lover's ship was wrecked and his returning was delayed, she succumbed to a great sadness and died. The goddess Hera took pity on her and transformed her into an almond tree." Another story was about Io who lost her love because of Venus's deception and became a violet. "Io was in love with the shepherd Artis. But Venus, who favored Artis, ordered Cupid to shoot a lead arrow at him to make him forget Io. As a result, Artis turned cold to Io. Unable to bear the heartbreak, Io soon died and Venus took pity on her and turned her into a violet." The number of stories about plants and their transformation was larger than the number of plants I knew. And all of them were stories about frustrated love.

No one had asked my brother to record these myths, but he must've had his reasons. *Did the manila envelope mean that he has finished his writing?* I leafed through the pages. I was right. "The End" was written at the bottom of page 253. The words seemed to be an omen embossed on the last page.

Where could he have possibly gone after finishing his writing? Hoping for some clue, I flipped through the manuscript. A story entitled "The Snowbell and the Pine" near the end caught my attention. I had a strong hunch that this story contained a special significance, as if it were a cryptic code that I had to crack. But the mystery was revealed as soon as I began reading the story. The first sentence read, "The male protagonist of this story is Woo-hyeon and Soon-mee has the female lead." This was clearly different from the myths about the transformations of trees and flowers; this story was his own creation, or his own confession. I quickly read the story.

"Woo-hyeon takes photos. He sees the world through his camera. To him photography is neither a hobby nor an art. It's a record of the objective facts and truths of a particular time and place. Photos are the most accurate eyes and the most honest voice to give a testimony of events. Through his photos, Woo-hyeon wants to be a confessor of his times. Soon-mee is his girlfriend. She sings songs while playing her guitar. Like every beautiful and noble love, their love also experiences a crisis. Woo-hyeon is no longer able to take photos. Because of the photos he took to record his times, his friends, who fought against an oppressive political power, were arrested by the ruthless ruler's cronies. Woo-hyeon himself is interrogated and tortured. Their interrogation is just a formality, but their torture is severe. Woo-hyeon feels that the investigation is just a façade for revenge. He is then forced into the military. There, he loses his legs. A hidden bomb exploded and flung his body into the air. And in midair he watched his legs tear into pieces. He knew then that his love was dead."

It was their story. But it didn't end there.

"After losing both his love and his will to live, Woo-hyeon goes into the forest and there he prays to be transformed into a tree. 'My lasting love and desire for Soon-mee is too much to bear. Please, take them away from me.' The god of the forest takes pity on him and grants his appeal. His body is covered with rough bark as he turns into a tree.

Learning that her lover has avoided her not because he doesn't love her but because he doesn't want to reveal his maimed body to her, Soon-mee wants to see Woo-hyeon again, but by then he is no longer human. Weeping, Soon-mee goes into the forest where Woo-hyeon used to take his walks. In tears, she sings for Woo-hyeon, the man she loved so much, the man she has never stopped loving even for a moment, but who is no longer a man. As she sings, branches of a tree sway. At first she thinks it's the wind that moves the tree. But as she continues singing, the tree's branches and roots slither toward her and wrap around her body. She detects the smell of her lover coming from the tree.

Realizing that her lover has become a tree, she also pleads to the god of the forest. 'Please, like my love, turn me into a tree. I wish to remain with my love and live here in this forest.' The forest god, a sympathizer of lovers, grants her plea. Not covered in rough bark, but instead retaining her velvety skin, she too becomes a tree.

The snowbell tree that Soon-mee was transformed into clings to Woo-hyeon's pine tree. Like arms, her branches hug his trunk and like legs, her roots are entwined with his. Even after changing their forms, their love and desire are indestructible. Now transformed into trees, Woo-hyeon and Soon-mee can now freely express themselves. They consummate their love as they had never been able to as humans. The desire felt by trees is greater than any human's and their love is more sincere. It was Woo-heon and Soon-mee's passionate desire and sincere love that transformed them both into trees."

When I reached this part of his story, I thought I might know where he had gone. Putting the manuscript back in the envelope and rushing out of his room, I shouted, "Mother, I think I know where he might be."

Mother followed behind me saying she wanted to come with me. But I picked up a flashlight from the hall closet and ran out of the house, leaving her behind. I wasn't completely sure that he had gone into the forest and even if he had gone to that spot upon finishing his writing project, it was so late at night now that it was unlikely for him to still be there. Nevertheless, after seeing the story of the snowbell and the pine tree, I had to check.

I recalled the night that I had accompanied my brother into the forest on the way back home from one of his motel visits. He had asked me to take him down the meandering, bumpy trail that skirted the King's tomb. And once there, in the darkness, he talked about a snowbell tree and a pine tree that I couldn't see.

"I can imagine the dense forest beyond the hedge," he had said. "I can imagine the tall trees competing to possess the sky and the deep caves that must be somewhere out there. And I can imagine shrubs and wild grasses entwined with each other and with the birds and insects and animals and the earth. And if I keep going deeper into the forest maybe I would find a gigantic ash tree there, propping up the sky. I wonder if I would see all that if I went deeper and deeper into the forest. I always wanted to go further in. Once there, I would also want to become part of the forest. I would want to touch the huge ash tree that not only props up the sky but also props up time."

He had seemed to be talking to himself. And I sensed that he had a strong yearning for something, but I couldn't figure out what it was. I knew now what he so ardently wished for.

I'm fearful of the forest at night; it's the world beyond logic, the world of spirits and witches. I'd never been in the forest at night alone. And if the flashlight wasn't able to clear away the darkness, it also wouldn't be able to clear away my fear. I called out my brother's name as I ran through the forest but my voice was muffled by the night. I wanted my words to shatter my fear of the darkness, but instead they only seemed to increase it.

Thinking I had arrived in the vicinity of the snowbell tree, I was forced to a halt. A fence that I had never noticed before blocked me from going further. On the other side of the fence, the forest was drenched in a deep darkness and submerged in a mysterious calmness. Indeed, darkness was the ruler of the night forest. It looked like an immense black hole with its ghastly mouth open wide. Only darkness existed there; I saw no snowbell or pine tree. Looking over the fence, my flashlight scanning the forest, I called out my brother's name. But the light couldn't disperse the stubborn particles of darkness and my voice was swallowed up by the forest. The only response was a bird flapping its wings as it soared up toward the sky. Startled, I stepped back. Shadows hanging from the trees intensified the eerie atmosphere. I pointed my flashlight to the ground.

If the dancing beam hadn't then fell on a shiny, silver object I would've walked away. But instead, I walked closer to it and saw that it was my brother's wheelchair, lopsided, with one wheel stuck in the mud. "Woo-hyeon!" I yelled out. But there was no reply. "Woo-hyeon!" I called out again, straightening the wheelchair. But I didn't see him anywhere.

Where could he be? I asked myself. But at least one thing was sure—he had come to the forest. I was surprised that he had made it here alone, and at night, but what really confused me was how he had disappeared after getting there in his wheelchair. I stared at the fence barring me from the forest. I remembered my brother saying that he wanted to go further into the forest and to become part of it. He also said that he dreamed of entering the forest and touching the huge ash tree that not only propped up the sky but also time. *It can't be,* I thought, not wanting to believe it. Even if the allure of the forest had been irresistible for him, the fence was made of barbed wire. There was an opening in the fence that a person could possibly fit through but it would be a difficult task even for a physically sound man. There was no way that my legless brother could have gotten through on his own. *But where is he? He must have made it through the hole in the fence, there's nowhere else he could be.* Before I shoved my body through the opening in the fence, I cleared my throat to dispel my fear. But it didn't leave me.

33

"Turn off the light," someone said. I hadn't expected him to be there so it took me a few moments to recognize the voice as my father's. I turned off the flashlight that had guided me through the darkness and then asked, "Who's there? Is Woo-hyeon with you?"

"It's me, your brother just fell asleep," Father said. As I moved closer to the sound of his voice I finally saw him, squatting near the ground like a black shadow.

"Father!" I cried out, surprised but glad to see him there.

The forest was quiet except for the occasional sound of a dry twig falling or the wretched cackle of a bird. But none of this really disturbed the silence of the night forest, not even the rustling of my steps. An uneasy stillness rose up majestically above all the small noises of the night.

Before spotting my father, I had stretched out an opening in the barbed wire fence and stepped through into the dark forest. I had felt as if I were entering the silence at the beginning of the world. To ease my fear I repeatedly called out my brother's name while slowly making my way through the trees but the forest absorbed my voice like a sponge. The silence so overwhelmed me that for a moment I forgot why I was there. The forest itself seemed to be the inside of a gigantic ash tree or a deep dark cave. That was why I was momentarily confused when I heard a voice obviously directed at me.

Leaning against the trunk of a thick tree, Father held my brother on his lap, gently caressing his head. The eerie setting looked like a scene from a movie. I felt as if my brother and Father were inside a vacuum and some unseen barrier separated them from me. And I didn't feel like it was permissible to enter their space, so I stopped.

I noticed Father was mumbling as he combed my brother's hair with his fingers. I couldn't hear him but I saw him moving his lips.

It looked like he was explaining something to my brother or giving him some fatherly advice. Who knows, maybe he was even singing him a lullaby. I couldn't see my brother's face, but I knew that he was at peace. Suddenly, I realized that my father's movements were familiar. This was the same way he had spoken to the leaves in the garden. He had tried to teach me then how to have a sincere love for plants. He told me to tell the plants "I love you" with a true heart. He had also said that plants know by instinct whether or not a person speaks the truth. False love doesn't bring any reaction. He said that to communicate with plants one must be truthful, and the same with people. At that moment in the forest, like some auditory hallucination, I thought I heard him say that to communicate with people, one should be truthful, the same as with plants. As when I had waited for my father in the garden while he communicated with the plants, I understood that I now had to wait for him while he communicated with my brother.

No longer relying on the flashlight, things began to faintly take shape in the darkness. Trees dangled their branches toward the ground, shielding my brother and Father like an umbrella. The trees looked not only protective but also menacing, not only keeping things out but also holding them in.

"He said he wanted to become a tree," Father said. His voice sounded as if it came from far away. Listening to him, I realized that I had wanted to tell someone that very thing for a long time: my brother wanted to be a tree. And it must've been the real reason for his obsession with the tree transformation myths.

Finally feeling like I was allowed to cross the threshold into their world, I asked Father whether he had brought my brother to the forest. My mother had said she'd sent Father out looking for my brother so I knew that they hadn't left home together. But I didn't see how my brother could have possibly gotten there by himself and I sensed an unusual closeness between the two of them.

"No, I didn't," Father answered, in a subdued tone. "I was on the way to the Lotus Flower Market to look for him," he said, "but I suddenly remembered that Woo-hyeon liked this place. So I came here first and saw his wheelchair at the end of the path. I didn't really believe that he could have gotten himself to the other side of the fence, but I wasn't sure. And soon afterwards, I found him here on the ground. His body was black and blue all over and stained with blood. It's a wonder he made it all the way here on his own. It seems that he wanted to be somewhere with no one around." Father continued to caress my brother's hair just as he had the plants in the garden.

A sudden sympathy for my brother surged in me. I had thought that I understood his suffering and sadness well enough but my understanding was partial and shallow. It wasn't so bad that my brother had given up searching for his purpose in this world. But what was truly serious was that he couldn't bear himself for having given up, and he suffered greatly because of it. Realizing that what he really wanted was to transcend reality, to leave it all behind, I felt ashamed. What he wanted more than anything was to transform his body; he had a burning desire to cast himself away and obliterate his very existence. I couldn't imagine a more desperate desire.

"He said that he wanted to be a tree," Father repeated. His voice fell into the dark forest with the softness of a flower petal. "When I picked him up in my arms, Woo-hyeon shook and cried. But I didn't wipe away his tears. I let him cry. I wanted his tears to purge him. I wished for his sadness to be dissolved in his tears and flushed from his body. Woo-hyeon told me that he wanted to be a tree. He repeated these very words in my arms, 'I want to become a tree.' So I told him that he's already a tree. If one dreams of becoming a tree, he already has a tree's soul, and if one already has a tree's soul, then the person is already a tree." Listening to Father speak, it was clear that he truly loved my brother.

"Let's go home. I'll carry him," I said finally. But my words sounded hollow. They were the words of someone who had never experienced great pain, pain that would require spiritual transcendence to overcome. My thoughts and actions had never truly stepped outside the boundaries of reality. This was what had caused my alienation from my family as well as my constant sense of inferiority.

"He's sleeping soundly. I think we should leave him alone till he wakes up," Father said. He didn't ask me to stay but he didn't tell me to go home, either. I began to worry about Mother, back home panicking, but I didn't feel right leaving my father and brother behind in the forest. Father mumbled something to my brother who in fact looked to be in a deep sleep. It was almost as if Father had entered my brother's dream and was conversing with him. I was once again an outsider.

34

I was no longer afraid of the forest at night. If you sit in the darkness long enough it becomes a luminous body. I sat next to my father and saw that his jacket covered my brother. I took mine off and put it around my father's shoulders, so thin that they looked like dry branches. I told him that I could hold my brother, but he shook his head. I had become familiar with the darkness, but the silence still made me uncomfortable.

After some time had passed, my father suddenly announced, "Your mother is pure." I wasn't sure how to respond to this announcement. Words swirled in my mind but I made an effort to contain them. What did he mean by this? Even though I had rejected the possibility that Father was the client who had asked me to tail my mother, I still couldn't shake off my suspicion, which had come to me one day, suddenly, like an epiphany, and never left. I had considered asking him directly, but I always backed out at the last moment. Was Father finally about to confess to me, here in this dark forest? *Please, don't do it,* I shouted inside my head. But I realized that the person who really wanted to talk was my father. Slowly, his words trickled out and sank into the night.

"I asked someone to hire you to follow your mother," he said, almost whispering. But since he was gazing at my brother and his hands were touching him, he appeared to be talking to him. Thinking that any reaction from me would be taken as putting pressure on him, I didn't say anything. But my heart thumped as I listened.

"Some time ago, a man came to see me," Father said. "He was a stooped and white-haired old man. I didn't know who he was until he introduced himself. He was someone who at one time worked for a man whom your mother had loved and had never stopped loving. He said that your mother's man had returned home from an overseas exile and was very ill with little time left to live. He said that the man hadn't told him anything but he sensed that he wanted to see your mother and his son. At first I didn't want to help him. To begin with, I didn't have any idea how to explain the whole story to you two, especially to Woo-hyeon. I felt that bringing it up would hurt you guys and it didn't seem like the right thing to do. I intended to carry it all to my grave … I especially worried that it would be too much for your brother if I brought another father into his life now. But, after three days of thinking about it, I decided to do what the old man wanted. I asked him, though, for some time in order to help both of you to understand and digest the situation. This happened right after you had started your business, Bees and Ants. I'm still not sure if it was the best idea, but I thought that if I hired you to follow your mother you would learn about the situation more gradually. I wanted you both to know our family secrets. I knew that your mother would go to Namcheon and that you would follow her and learn about the relationship between her and the man, and I would then wait for you and your brother to ask me for an explanation. And I thought this would be a better way for you to learn the truth. So I asked the old man to act as your client. Of course, he won't call you again. There isn't any reason for him to call you now. And incidentally, I didn't know that your mother's man was that sick. It was wrong of me to have waited."

I wondered if my brother had already heard the entire story from my father and the thought crossed my mind that he might even be able to hear us as he slept. "That means you knew about the relationship between Mother and …" I couldn't finish the sentence. I didn't want to ask him anything that would make him uncomfortable. But he seemed determined to reveal everything, something very unusual for my father.

"When I met your mother, I was twenty-five and she was twenty-one," Father said, ready to make his confession. "When your mother started working at the Dandelion, I was already working there. I was the chef. When I saw your mother, my heart sank. It was the first time I had felt that way about a woman. At first sight I knew I would fall in love with her." His voice trembled slightly but he continued.

"And since then, I've never stopped loving her, even for a moment, and it's the same with your mother—she never stopped loving the man. I was blind to women other than your mother and she was blind to men other than her man." Father's voice lowered and his face looked forlorn. "But it didn't matter to me; I was a happy man just loving her. Your mother was the first and only person who taught me how much happiness can come from loving another person. And that's enough to make your mother precious to me. I'm not sure if you knew this, but your mother gave birth to your brother at that magical spot on the cliff in Namcheon."

Father then paused for a moment, as if lost in recollection. "It was your mother who wanted to deliver her child there. And I was the one who drove her to the house when it was time. And I helped with the delivery and care of the newborn baby. Your mother didn't want me to help, but I did it anyway. Your mother pushed me away in fact, but I insisted on staying . . . I just couldn't leave them there. We stayed there for a month as she recovered. There was plenty of seafood in the ocean so every day I cooked and prepared meals for her, and I was the happiest man in the world. To both your mother and me, Namcheon is an unforgettable place. She had her happiest times there and so did I. I was determined to stay beside her, regardless of the fact that she loved someone else. It was my pleasure to protect her and my duty as well. Even when I felt that your mother didn't love me, it never became a reason for me not to love her.

Later on, I often took trips to Namcheon alone. Your mother didn't go but I did. I was happy there but she wasn't. Eventually, I began to notice a palm tree growing from the cliff. It was a miracle to me that a tropical plant could survive in a foreign climate and soil. And that became another reason for my trips—to see this miracle unfold. For a while the tree was only as high as my knee, but it soon reached my height, then double, triple, and quadruple my height, and so on. And every time I saw it I expected some kind of miracle to happen to me too. But it was just wishful thinking. Understand, I loved only your mother, even before I began living with her, and your mother has loved only the man, even after she began living with me." Father smiled faintly and paused to collect himself before he continued. "But your mother is pure. It might seem incomprehensible, but I think what I love most about her is her pureness."

I wasn't quite sure what he meant when he said that Mother was pure but I felt like I could empathize with him. Knowing someone is different from understanding everything they say and understanding the meaning of someone's words isn't enough to know someone. I had once pitied my father when I imagined that he wasn't happy in his relationship with Mother. I had never realized that my father's heart was so wide open, like the broad fronds of the palm tree whose roots hugged the ocean. I guess I had always sensed that he was different but I never understood until that moment that my father had the soul of a tree.

"Father," I said, in a more affectionate tone than usual. He lifted his arm and gently placed it on my head. It felt like the branch of a leafy tree. As if I had been waiting for his touch, my body leaned softly against his chest. His hand rubbed my hair. I realized then that my father's affection was something I had wanted for a long time. Burying my head in his chest, I heard not only my heart thumping but also my father's and brother's. The night forest now felt familiar and cozy. Soon I thought I could almost make out the giant ash tree that not only props up the sky but also time, a tree that's been around since the beginning of the world. I knew then that the tree my brother wanted to see wasn't in the forest — it existed only in people's hearts. The tree cannot be found in any forest — the tree is something we become. My heartrate returned to normal and I felt at peace.

35

After returning from the forest, my brother was bedridden for two days. The doctor said that he needed to rest. And Mother didn't leave his side the whole time. It was the first time I can ever remember her staying home for so long. I was in a rush to return to Namcheon since Soon-mee was there alone. If everything had worked as planned, I would've driven back with my brother. But he couldn't travel in his state and it would have been useless for me to return alone. But I soon remembered that there was a phone in the cliff house and that Mother had given me the number when she'd asked me to bring my brother to her. I had lost the paper with the number on it, and I wasn't even sure if the phone would still be in service, but I decided I had to ask mother for it.

"What do you need it for?" she asked me.

"Oh, no particular reason," I answered. But this didn't satisfy her.

"No particular reason? Who would be there now?" she mumbled, looking at me quizzically.

"Do you have it?" I was trying to avoid any further questions.

"Of course I have it, but I don't think anyone's there to answer the phone. I heard that the last occupant, the driver, left the house and came back to Seoul," she said, walking to the kitchen.

She prepared her tea and then sat at the kitchen table to drink it. "Why don't you make some for Father too," I asked on an impulse. It sounded like the suggestion had come from somewhere else, like somebody inside me had told me what to say. I had never seen my mother prepare tea for my father. They always ate, slept, and had tea separately. So asking her to make tea for him was an odd request.

"Mother, do you know that even after dozens of years Father cherishes the month he spent with you in Namcheon, the time when he cooked and prepared meals for you, as the happiest time in his life?" My words flew out before I could even arrange them in my head.

But Mother didn't react. She didn't even turn around. I only heard the jingling sound of her teaspoon hitting the cup. She must've been embarrassed by what I'd said, but I just couldn't stop the words from coming. "Father truly loves you and always has," I said. The kettle on the stove whistled. I soon regretted being so presumptuous. But I couldn't take back the words that I had already spoken.

"You're talking as if I disliked your father," Mother said, calmly, after a slight pause, but she still didn't turn around and face me.

"Oh no, that's not what I meant," I said, waving my hand for emphasis.

But Mother continued. "I know that your father cares for me and remembers fondly the time we spent at Namcheon. And I know your father is a very nice man. If I hadn't met him, I don't know how my life would've turned out . . . I probably wouldn't even be alive today. He's my Good Samaritan. And I've often thought of him as my guardian angel. No, it's not that I don't love him; it's that I have a guilty conscience about him. And I don't try to avoid him. It's just that I'm a little restrained in his presence. Maybe it's hard for you to understand this, but that's our way of loving each other." Mother then finally turned around and looked directly at me. She seemed to be searching my face for understanding. She filled a teacup and placed it in front of me. "Please, take it to your father."

"Mother, if you take it, he would be very happy," I said, looking down at the cup of green tea. Mother closed her eyes for a second but soon opened them. I was pressing the issue but I didn't think that I was doing anything wrong.

"In front of your father . . . I'm ashamed of myself. I've lived my life with my head hung in shame. I don't have any shame when I face other people, but I feel nothing but shame when it comes to your father." Mother's eyes were closed by the time she had finished her confession. I thought I could finally begin to grasp their way of loving each other.

"Mother!" I called out, but I couldn't say anything more. Instead, I picked up the teacup. *Every love is different,* I said to myself. *Love is love, but the way people experience it is different. One hundred people love in one hundred different ways. So there's no love that isn't special,* I thought as I walked toward my father's room with his tea.

When I returned to the kitchen, Mother was having her tea alone at the table. I sat down in front of her.

"Tell me why you wanted the phone number," she said, wrapping her hands around the teacup.

I had planned to keep the trip a secret. I was going to take my brother to Namcheon to meet Soon-mee without anyone knowing. But I questioned this. Did I need to hide it from my mother? "Someone's there," I told her. She looked at me suspiciously and asked who it was. "Someone you know . . . it's Soon-mee," I said.

This information must have surprised her. She narrowed her eyes like she was trying hard to figure out what was going on. But soon, as if acknowledging her inability to do so, she asked, "Why . . . how?"

"She's waiting for Woo-hyeon. I took her there," I answered.

Mother stared at me for a moment with the same puzzled look before giving me the phone number. As I left the table Mother cautiously asked, "Do you think it'll be okay?"

I understood what her question meant. And I told her in a purposely cheerful voice, "I'll be fine."

I immediately called Namcheon. After a few rings, the operator informed me that the number was no longer in service. I tried again, but no luck. Standing behind me, Mother's eyes were asking what was happening. "The number didn't go through," I told her.

"What should we do then?" She seemed disappointed.

"Do you think Woo-hyeon can travel to Namcheon tomorrow?" I asked her. "Well, I guess," she said.

36

Father cooked. No one asked him to. Actually, I had made a big show about preparing dinner myself and he decided to take over. Mother had given the housekeeper three days off since she was staying home to take care of my brother until he recovered. So upon returning from the grocery store I took out a cookbook and walked back and forth between my father's room and the kitchen, saying that I was going to cook *lajogy* and asking him how long I should soak dried mushrooms, how big I should cut the chicken pieces, and what the best temperature for frying chicken was. Eventually, Father came into the kitchen and put on an apron. This was exactly what I had hoped would happen, and my plan worked perfectly. I knew that my family wanted to be closer but no one knew what to do about it. I was the only person up to the task so I had to take action. My parents had just begun to open their hearts and expose what had been sealed inside for so long. If we missed this opportunity we might not get another one in the future. So I decided to use Father's cooking skills to help bind our family together.

After looking through the grocery items I'd brought home, Father asked me what I was cooking. So I showed him the recipes for *lajogy* and *palbochae* in the cookbook. I saw him smile mischievously. He checked my grocery bag again and also the refrigerator and then jotted down more things for me to get. I returned to the store to get the items he'd requested: tofu, beef, mushrooms, dropwort, croaker, broccoli, cauliflower, sweet pea, oysters, and milk. I also bought a bottle of wine. Father's hands were swift and dexterous while cooking. He was the chef, only asking me to do some simple tasks, such as peeling garlic or trimming vegetables. Mother must've known what was happening in the kitchen but she didn't come out of her room.

Dinner was a feast. Father had prepared *lajogy*, steamed croaker, tofu stew, and oyster soup. The many dishes arranged on the table looked like a work of art, too beautiful to eat. My mother and brother seemed to think the same; standing at the table, they were at a loss for words. There was no mistaking the expression on my mother's face—she was touched.

"Well, lady and gentlemen, let's enjoy these delicious gourmet dishes that the world's best chef has to offer," I said playfully, filling our glasses with wine. "This is a Chateaux Ausone. As you may know, it is made from grapes grown in Saint-Emilion in Bordeaux, France. The wine was named after Ausone, the poet and Governor-General of Imperial Rome, who once ruled the area." I closed my speech with a toast. Awkwardly, they all held up their glasses. "Father, do you have any wise words to offer?" I asked. He blushed as we waited for him to say something. My brother and mother were especially attentive.

Father cleared his throat a couple of times, as if preparing to deliver a big speech, but all he said was, "I love you all." His voice was deep and it seemed to resonate through every corner of our home.

"Mother, it's your turn now," I said.

"It's all so ceremonial," she said, hesitating a bit. "But I like it, maybe we can eat together from now on." Her voice tapered off and so the last part of her speech was almost indecipherable.

"Now it's your turn, Woo-hyeon," I said to my brother. He slowly looked around, first to Father, then Mother, and finally me, and then he closed his eyes. A teardrop trickled down his cheek. I hurriedly tried to save the situation; I didn't want any sadness at the dinner table. "This wine weighs in our hands. And it isn't for holding, it's for drinking. Let's toast!" I said. I touched glasses with my father, then Mother, and then my brother, the wine dancing to the sounds of clinking crystal. Father and Mother also toasted each other.

"This is steamed croaker and that is *lajogy*. And this right in front of me is tofu stew, and the dish in front of us is oyster soup. But Father's works of art aren't for display but for eating. Please, help yourselves," I said. Everybody grinned. I knew that they appreciated my effort. I also appreciated their effort to smile at my bad jokes. It was clear that we were all making an effort.

I don't remember what the dishes tasted like; to me, the meal was symbolic. It was hard to relish the food while preoccupied with so many emotions. Our appetite succumbed to other things, mine to anticipation and Mother's to memory. I saw the memory of a certain time slow her hand and moisten her eyes as she spooned oyster soup into her mouth. While we were in the kitchen cooking, Father had said that he'd prepared oyster soup many times when he was taking care of Mother after she gave birth in Namcheon. He said that she liked his oyster soup so much that he went out to pick fresh oysters from the rocks almost every day at low tide. Emotions as deep as the ocean must have swelled up in Mother that night at the dinner table.

37

I lay in bed that night thinking about the trip I would take to Namcheon with my brother. Soon-mee, the woman I loved, was there
waiting for him. I loved Soon-mee the way that my father loved
my mother. But she loved my brother, just as my mother loved another man. But just as it can't be said that Mother doesn't love Father, it also can't be said that Soon-mee doesn't love me. I tossed all
night. So many things had happened in the last several days that
it seemed like a thousand years had passed. I felt like I was a thousand years old or like a thousand layers of sediment had piled up in
my heart and in my head. When I finally fell asleep around dawn I
had a dream so vivid that it seemed real. And it was like a preview
of what was to come.

The setting of my dream is Namcheon. The ocean waves cease-
lessly strike the cliff. A gigantic tree stands at the edge of the cliff, a
tree that looks like it has existed since the beginning of the world and
props up not only the sky but also time. Under the tree, a woman
stands. She is naked and pure. Her name is Soon-mee. My brother stands in front of her. He's holding the camera I bought for him,
not only because I once stole his camera and caused him to abandon photography, but also because I wanted him to reconnect with
this world. But those weren't the only reasons. Most of all I thought
that if my brother picked up his camera again, my feelings of guilt
might be diminished. I know now that I will never be absolutely
free of my guilt. Some misdeeds are as indelible as a tattoo.

But now, with his camera in hand, my brother's face lights up
after a long and wretched period of darkness. Soon-mee's naked
purity is recorded by the camera through which my brother once
again sees the world. And the world is one of love. From a hill in
the distance I sit watching, as I've done before. It's a scene I wanted

to see. Every time the camera's shutter clicks, my heart also clicks. And the palm tree that props up time as well as the sky stands firm against the blowing wind. The sun turns the ocean's surface into a million teardrops which glitter like gemstones. But I don't cry.

About the Author

LEE SEUNG-U is a professor of Korean literature at Chosun University. His first novel, *A Portrait of Erysichton*, received the New Writers Award from *Korean Literature Monthly*. His novel *The Reverse Side of Life* was a finalist for the Prix Femina and is available in English.

About the Translators

INRAE YOU VINCIGUERRA has, along with her husband, LOUIS VINCIGUERRA, translated four Korean novels into English.